The Lumberjack's Unwelcome Christmas Bride

Cheryl Wright

Copyright

THE LUMBERJACK'S UNWELCOME CHRISTMAS BRIDE
(Unwelcome Brides Series – Book Two)

Copyright ©2024 by Cheryl Wright

Small Town Romance Publications

Dedication

To Margaret Tanner, my very dear friend and fellow author, for her enduring encouragement and friendship.

To Alan, my husband of almost fifty years, who has been a relentless supporter of my writing and dreams for many years.

To You, my wonderful readers, who encourage me to continue writing these stories. It is such a joy knowing so many of you enjoy reading my stories as much as I love writing them for you.

Table of Contents

Chapter One

Mountain Pass – 1880s

Emily Bishop awoke from what felt like a drug induced stupor.

She had no idea where she was, or how she got there. What Emily did know, was she was cold. In fact, she was frozen to the bone, and couldn't stop shaking. It was also pitch black. Even if she managed to remove her bindings, she couldn't find the way out. Not in this lack of light.

Trying to stand, it became apparent she was bound, both hands and feet. It greatly impaired her ability to get up off the cold, snow-covered ground. Emily tried to call out, but found her mouth had been filled with…what she didn't know. Some form of material perhaps.

Whatever it was, it made breathing difficult.

Distressed and panicked, she tried to slow her heart rate. It was beating so fast, Emily felt light-headed. She lifted her hands to her face to brush away her tears. Her mind began to clear. If she could lift her hands, she could remove whatever impeded her breathing.

Slowly, carefully, she pulled the rag from her mouth. Emily glanced about. Still unsure how she arrived in this bleak, dark corner of the forest, Emily felt defeated. She closed her eyes after deciding to let herself slip away. No one would find her here. She was certain her whereabouts was completely unknown to everyone except Lonnie Jacobson and his criminal brothers. Or perhaps he acted alone.

When Lonnie kidnapped her from the stagecoach he'd robbed, Emily didn't know what to expect. He told her she would be his slave, but didn't elaborate. The rest of his gang tried to stop him, but he went ahead with his plans.

From the moment he saw her, Lonnie told Emily she was beautiful. His cold fingers seem to match his ice cold heart. He didn't care about Emily. Wasn't interested in knowing she was expected by her elderly aunt. Instead he held a gun to her head and threatened to shoot if she didn't come willingly.

Emily shivered at the memory.

With her mind finally clearing, Emily recalled the exact moment everything changed. Out of the blue Lonnie slapped her. It was enough to knock her to the floor. In that moment, she feared for her life.

Her heart pounding, and her entire body shaking, Emily shivered as Lonnie said he was tired of her. He needed to find a different woman, one who was much more beautiful than her.

It was in that moment Emily knew her life was in danger.

~*~

It was daylight when she awoke again. She was still shivering from the snow. Overnight the snow became heavier. Or perhaps it only felt that way because it landed on top of her. Wearing a thin cotton gown, and little else, Emily was chilled to the bone.

She'd had a dream when she slept fitfully during the night. Or perhaps it was a nightmare. Lonnie was there, along with his four brothers. They held her down and tied her up. It was Lonnie who shoved the rag into her mouth. He muttered something she couldn't decipher.

Emily saw herself being thrown into a wagon. Her aches and pains, not to mention bruises and scrapes, confirmed her belief. The nightmare was her recollection of how she was treated. It was far from a figment of her imagination.

Not one to cry easily, Emily allowed herself that release. After all, she would slip into the afterlife soon enough. She couldn't survive out here.

Especially the way she was dressed. Her cries turned into sobs, and her energy was drained.

Glancing about, Emily watched the sun rise. It might be between the trees, but it was still beautiful. She swiped at her face again, and tried to compose herself, but couldn't. Her wish now, was to slip away quietly and without pain.

She closed her eyes, and let herself relax into the inevitable.

Chapter Two

Tobias Harrison stopped what he was doing. It was peaceful here early in the morning. The sounds of the birds twittering helped calm his nerves. There was always the possibility he might not make it out alive.

This time of year, his customers wanted trees for Christmas. Not huge, small enough to display in their homes. He knew exactly where to find them. As he lifted his axe, ready to swing at the pine tree he was about to fell, Tobias paused.

The birdsong stopped, and without warning, hundreds of birds ascended to the sky – all at once.

The birdlife were used to him, and accustomed to Tobias's work here each day. It definitely wasn't anything he did that frightened them.

He wasn't alone.

Axe in his hand, Tobias walked toward the curious sound. It wasn't something he'd heard before, and that bothered him. There were no other lumberjacks in the area, so it wasn't that, either.

Hand on his gun, he cautiously ambled toward the sound, ensuring he made no noise. What he found was totally unexpected, but Tobia knew he had to do something.

He lifted the unconscious woman, and carried her back to his cottage. It could be too late already, but he couldn't leave her out here to die.

It wasn't until he held her in his arms, he noticed the bindings on her hands and feet. And the bruise across her face. This was far more serious than he first imagined.

Tobias sighed. He would have to get the sheriff involved.

Pulling a thick blanket up over the stranger, Tobias felt as though he had intruded on her privacy. What he'd really done, and deep down, Tobias knew it, was save her life. He'd stripped the woman of her wet clothes, and placed her on a pallet close to the fire. It was the only way he could bring her back from the brink.

Tobias knew he should have taken her to town. Doc would have fixed her up good, but it was over an hour away. She didn't have that long. How long she had lay in the snow, fully exposed, he had no idea. What Tobias did know was he'd found her in time.

At least it seemed that way. Once she awoke, and was well enough, he'd take her to town.

It was the right thing to do. Let the doc look her over, and inform the sheriff. Then he could wipe his hands of her. Having a woman in his cottage, or his life, was not what Tobias wanted. He preferred to live alone, and live the way he wanted. He only hoped, when she came around, this woman didn't try to insinuate herself into his life.

Why was he even thinking this way? She was beautiful, there was no doubt. Even in her disheveled and damaged state, Tobias could see that. Who would do something so barbaric? It had him fuming.

No doubt it was someone who needed to be taught a lesson. A shiver went down his spine. It was not his business and not his problem. Tobias had done his part, and that was saving the woman's life.

He strolled to the kitchen. It had been a difficult morning, and he needed coffee. Tobias poured himself a mug, then glanced across at the stranger in his sitting room. What would he do with her? He couldn't leave her alone to fetch the sheriff and the doctor. Anything might happen. It wasn't as though he'd only be gone a few minutes. His cottage was at the edge of the forest, since that's where he spent much of his days.

Sitting at the kitchen table, he pondered his dilemma. What if she needed immediate medical attention? He couldn't take her butt naked as she was now. Nor did he anticipate redressing her in wet clothes to take her into town.

He glanced across at the clothes he placed near the fire to dry, after he'd roughly cleaned them. If she awoke before they dried, he'd have to lend her some clothes.

The thought made him chuckle. She wasn't tall. In fact, Tobias estimated she wouldn't even reach his shoulder.

Glancing down into the mug of hot liquid, Tobias knew something had to be done. The problem was, he wasn't sure what.

Which was even more reason to take her to town. The thought filled him with dread. Instead, he would go outside. Chopping wood for the fire always seemed to clear his mind. Tobias pulled on his thick coat, and shoved his hat on his head. Pulling his gloves from his pocket, Tobias braced himself against the cold.

Chapter Three

Emily awoke with a fright. Her eyes roamed around the room. Exactly where was she? It was warm, she knew that much. Especially underneath the thick blanket.

She had no idea how she got here. The last thing she remembered was waking up and finding herself bound and lying in the snow. Her situation was dire, she knew that much. Emily remembered crying, and finally, sobbing. After that, she didn't recall a thing.

She pulled her hands out from under the blanket. They were no longer bound. Was it another nightmare? Focusing her gaze on her wrists, Emily confirmed she hadn't dreamed it. Her wrists held the proof of her belief. Throwing back the blanket to check her feet, Emily gasped. Her feet were free, but she was naked.

Her heart pounded. How did that happen? Who undressed her and why? She closed her eyes, trying to bury the awful thoughts running through her mind.

Tears filled her eyes. Her life was already worth nothing. Her reputation would be ruined, and she could never marry. What decent man would marry a woman who was no longer a virgin?

The door suddenly opened and she quickly pulled the blanket back over herself. It took a moment to realize whomever undressed her already saw her in all her nakedness. She silently prayed that person was a woman.

"Ah, you're awake. Good."

Emily shuddered at the sound of a man's voice. She cringed, and pulled the blanket up over her face. "Where am I?" Emily asked, her voice barely audible.

The giant of a man carried an arm full of logs. He walked over to the firebox and dropped them in it. "I'm Tobias Harrison," he said, walking toward her. "I found you earlier this morning, in the forest."

Emily had lost all sense of time. She could have been laying there for days, for all she knew.

He sat on a nearby chair. "What is your name," he asked gently.

Not understanding whhy, Emily trusted this man. "Emily," she whispered. "Emily Bishop." She stared at him. Tobias Harrison appeared trustworthy, but who really knew? "Please tell me it wasn't you who undressed me."

His face went red, and Emily's heart sank. "I had no choice. You were close to death, and almost frozen solid. If I'd left you in those wet clothes, you wouldn't be here now."

Emily felt the heat rise up from her neck to her cheeks. Never had she been so embarrassed in her life. Although she understood why he'd done it, that didn't mean she had to like it. There was nothing she could do but nod.

And shrug her shoulders as though it didn't matter.

"The kettle is boiled. Would you prefer tea or coffee?"

She couldn't look him in the eye knowing this man had completely undressed her. "Tea, please," she said, staring at the roaring fire.

It was then she heard him chuckle. "There's no need to be embarrassed. It had to be done was all." He strolled into the kitchen and returned minutes later with a mug of tea and a large slice of pound cake on a small tray.

With the blanket wrapped around herself, Emily sat on the sofa. She wasn't sure how she could drink tea and hold up the blanket at the same time. It was a dilemma.

"I'll return shortly," Tobias said, then left the room. He returned quickly, holding a nightshirt. "It isn't much, and probably far too big, but it will keep you covered and protect your modesty," he told her, then left the room without another word.

Emily stared at the garment. Did she really want to wear it? It was clear to her it belonged to Tobias. She was in two minds – one was to refuse to wear it, but the sensible part of her brain told her she had little choice. Emily quickly donned the oversized cotton nightshirt before her host returned.

It felt better having something covering her, but made her wonder how long it would take for her clothes to dry. "You can come back," she called out, hoping Tobias could hear her from here. Emily wasn't certain she wanted to wander about in his nightshirt, with no other garment to cover her.

Glancing down at herself, Emily could see the shape of her waist, her breasts, and oh my goodness, the flimsy material covered little.

She huddled under the blanket once more, holding it up to her chin. Tobias entered, and frowned. "Is something wrong?" he asked. His concern evident.

"It's…" Should she even say the words?

Tobias stepped toward her, and instead of moving close to her, sat down on the same chair he'd been on earlier. "Tell me," he demanded gently.

Emily sighed. Her predicament became more embarrassing by the minute. "It…it shows everything." Her voice was a whisper – she hoped he hadn't heard her.

His eyebrows rose. Then he shook his head and left the room. It seemed like forever before he returned and Emily couldn't help but wonder why.

"It's probably too large, but it's thick and warm," he said, handing a man's robe to her.

Tobias was gone before she had a chance to speak. It was clear he wasn't used to company.

Chapter Four

How could he have not realized the nightshirt was so flimsy? Tobias admonished himself, but knew it was because he mostly wore only drawers to bed. It had been years since he'd worn nightshirts. He tried to remember the reason, and decided they must have been too thin to bother.

Living alone meant it didn't matter. But now he had a guest, and would need to be more careful. Hopefully, come tomorrow, her clothes would be completely dry. That being the case, Tobias would hand her over to the sheriff.

She could be his problem.

It still bothered him Emily had been dumped in the forest and left for dead. If he hadn't heard her sobbing, she would still be out there. It could have been days, weeks, or even months before she was found.

It was criminal. There was no other way to describe it. He couldn't imagine how anyone could do such a thing to another person. He knew outlaw gangs could be brutal, but Emily didn't seem the type to be involved with outlaws.

He had a stew on the stove, and stirred it. The action was calming. The warmth from the woodstove was comforting. It wasn't often he had visitors to his cottage, and Tobias preferred it that way. Answer to no one, that was his motto.

He spun around at the movement behind him.

"Thank you," she said quietly. "For everything." She licked her lips, and Tobias knew she had more to say. "I'll be out of your hair as soon as my clothes are dry."

Tobias frowned. "I'll take you to the sheriff's office in the morning. Your clothes should be ready by then." He turned back to the pot on the stove and stirred it again. The less he spoke, the happier he was.

Although Tobias had to admit, having Emily here was nice. He rarely got to talk to other people. He'd always liked it that way, but her company was making him think otherwise.

He shook himself mentally. Tobias was not interested in other people. They always caused problems. From the little he knew, she was mixed up in a heap of trouble. That meant *she* was trouble, and it was the last thing he needed.

"I…I don't think that's a good idea," she whispered, then turned away and headed back to the sitting room.

What was she running from? Or most importantly, who wanted her dead? It was clear to Tobias she needed the sheriff involved. Except Emily didn't want to tell the sheriff.

Trying to absorb it all, Tobias was confused. Someone had tried to kill her. Didn't Emily understand it was the case? Perhaps she had blocked it from her memory. He shook his head, trying to clear his mind. If they did it once, would they come back and ensure they'd succeeded? He hoped not. She seemed a nice person, but also very naïve. He stirred the stew again, then followed her the few steps to the sitting room.

The fire was beginning to burn down. He squatted down and threw a few more logs on the fire. Luckily, he'd chopped the wood earlier. The snow was even heavier now. "Blasted snow," he mumbled to himself. Tobias knew it was a sure sign they wouldn't make it to town tomorrow.

The closer they got to Christmas, the heavier the snow. It was the reason he'd been out so early. His customers were already wanting to buy Christmas trees and logs for their fires before the cold really set in. Tobias didn't blame them. He did the same thing.

He poked at the logs with the metal tool he bought for that very reason. Sparks flew, then settled. The heat brought him comfort, and he hoped it was doing the same for his unexpected guest. It wasn't that he didn't like her. It was more along the lines of him not being a welcoming host. He vowed long ago not to marry, and in the process, keep his distance from women. Now he had one in his house. One he had stripped naked to save her life.

He shook his head in despair as a thought entered his mind. The fact he'd removed her clothes without her consent – did that mean he had compromised Emily Bishop? Tobias groaned. Would the sheriff arrest him? All he did was try to save her life.

This was one of the very reasons he was unwelcoming when it came to strangers in his home.

~*~

It was clear his unwelcome guest was scared, although Emily wouldn't admit it. That meant Tobias could not leave her alone. If he hadn't stumbled across her in the forest, she would be dead by now. He had no doubt.

She still needed to recover, although Emily denied it, and said she was fine. He wasn't a doctor, of course he wasn't, but Tobias knew better. She could have frostbite at the very least. His intent was to take her to the doctor and the sheriff in the morning. Provided the snow didn't ruin his plans.

"I'm clean out of bread," he said, knowing he'd had time to make more before this. His guest had distracted Tobias, but it couldn't be helped.

"I can make biscuits," she said, her voice still unsure. "Provided you have the ingredients," she added.

He grinned. "I always have ingredients. We are isolated here as you've probably realized." Tobias grimaced. When did he go from being one person, to the pair being *we*? He hoped Emily hadn't noticed. Except the way her lips curled, he was certain she had.

"Point me in the right direction," she said firmly, then followed the direction he'd pointed.

Tobias left her alone while he set the table, then checked the fire again. He'd already refilled the cookstove earlier. Otherwise the stew would not have cooked as well as it had.

Emily resurfaced with her arms full of flour, butter and milk. "I couldn't find the eggs," she said, sounding defeated. He took the ingredients from her and placed them on the countertop.

"They are over here," Tobias told her. "With everything that's happened today, my routine was messed up."

She chewed on her bottom lip. "I'm sorry. I'll try to make it up to you."

Studying her, Tobias wasn't sure why Emily was apologizing. None of this was her fault. "You have nothing to apologize for," he told her firmly. Then reached into the cupboard and pulled out a large bowl and a flat tray. Supper could be interesting, he decided. Especially not knowing what sort of cook she was.

It wasn't long before the biscuits were in the oven. The aroma coming from the kitchen was enticing. Tobias didn't often make stew, but he'd thrown it together after he'd brought her home. Knowing she would need to eat well to keep up her strength was the deciding factor. Emily placed the butter in the middle of the table, and pulled plates from the cupboard. He tried to stop her since she was still in a weakened state, but Emily insisted.

The moment the biscuits came out of the oven, he knew they would be the best he'd ever eaten. Left to his own devices, Tobias didn't do much in the way of cooking. He made the most basic of meals. Not particularly nutritious, but enough to keep his belly full. Stew was a rare treat.

"They look good," he told her. "And they smell delicious."

She had rarely smiled since arriving here, but she did so now. "Thank you," she said. "Perhaps wait until you try them. I'm not the best cook in the world."

Tobias doubted that. His cottage was rarely filled with enticing aromas as it was today, but he wasn't complaining. Placing the still hot biscuits on a plate, she added them to the center of the table. Tobias dished out the stew, and placed a bowl for each of them on the table. "Tuck in," he said, hoping she would begin to eat first. Emily seemed reluctant. "I cannot start until you do," he said. If his mother was here, she would not be happy about his lack of manners should he eat before any woman sitting at his table.

Emily's eyebrows rose. Then she nodded, and lifted the fork to her mouth. "Wonderful," she said, then reached for a biscuit.

Not understanding the reason, Tobias felt contented. He was filled with warmth, but knew it had nothing to do with the heat from the fire. What he did know, was his life was different now, but he wasn't sure why.

Chapter Five

Emily ate slowly as she contemplated her future. Why she didn't realize earlier Lonnie would eventually want to eliminate her, she would never know. Her naivety had almost cost her life. Her only saving grace was Tobias.

If he hadn't found her when he did, who knew what would have happened?

A shudder went through her. Emily knew exactly what would have happened, and as much as she didn't want to admit it, knew for certain she would be dead now.

What's worse, her body may not have been found for days, or even weeks. If she hadn't given in to her emotions, she would still be lying out there in the snow. At the time, Emily knew she had nothing more to lose, and let the flood gates open. As it turned out, it saved her life.

She glanced up at Tobias and studied him. He was a kind man, but he seemed to prefer to keep his distance. Not only from Emily, but from everyone.

"The biscuits are good," he said, watching her as he spoke. "The best I've had." A slight smile poked through his lips. Did that mean he preferred not to smile? That he didn't like anyone to push through his armor?

"The stew is good too," Emily told him. "It warms the soul." And the body, she wanted to add. His home was small, but cozy. She felt at home here, except for not having her own clothes. Tomorrow they should be properly dry. Heat filled her face as Emily recalled Tobias had removed her wet clothes. All of them. In doing so, he had saved her life, but she still had mixed feelings about it.

Tobias chuckled. It was the first time she'd ever heard him make such a sound. From her perspective, he was a loner who did not like people around him. He also seemed to have a sadness about him. Was he miserable because he was lonely, or had something happened to make him this way? She would probably never know.

"I probably should have made dessert," Tobias muttered under his breath, his words barely audible.

"No need on my account," Emily told him. "I am grateful for the stew, and a warm place to stay." She wasn't sure what he was thinking, or how long he thought she would be here, but her next words surprised even Emily. "I'll be out of your hair as soon as my clothes are dry."

Frowning, Tobias put down his cutlery. "Where will you go?" he asked gruffly. "Your life is in danger."

On it's own accord, a gasp left Emily's mouth. Of course he was right. She had no money, no clothes, and nowhere to live. Lonnie had taken all of that from her when he decided to dispose of her like a piece of garbage.

Tears filled her eyes. Emily shook her head trying to block the memory of the moment the outlaw gang had turned on her. Lonnie's hands were around her throat, but one of his brothers pulled him away. He had a better idea. One that wouldn't lead the sheriff back to them.

Hot tears rolled down her face. What they'd done to her was unforgiveable.

Tobias was quickly by her side, his arms around her, holding Emily close. She didn't deserve to be treated the way Lonnie had treated her.

In his arms, Emily felt safe. Comforted and safe. This giant of a man cared about her, even if he did keep his distance. Except Emily knew, come tomorrow morning, weather permitting, he would hand her over to the sheriff. That way Tobias no longer had to deal with her.

Her heart thudded. Why did she say anything about leaving? Now Tobias would expect her to go the moment her clothes were dry. Hopefully he would drive her to town, otherwise she might find herself in the same situation again. Walking through heavy snow was not conducive to good health, especially when the township was so far away.

A thought struck her, and it almost took her breath away. "Do…" Emily closed her eyes momentarily. When she opened them again, she was staring into Tobias's eyes. "Do you think Lonnie would have hung around to ensure I was…" She couldn't bring herself to say the word, even though she thought it.

"No. No, I don't," Tobias said quickly. His quiet voice and the gentle way he said it made Emily feel assured of her safety. At least for now.

She studied his face. Not that she really knew this man, but his words contradicted his expression. Worry covered his face, and creased the corners of his eyes. Still, having him there with her helped quell her fears.

Emily lifted her hand and caressed his cheek. His hand covered hers. Moments later he pulled it away. "We can't do this," he said softly. "Tomorrow I'll drive you into town."

In other words, he didn't want her there, and didn't want to have any sort of feelings for her. Well, that could work both ways. Emily quickly stood, then gathered up their soiled dishes, and placed them in the bowl Tobias used to do the dishes. She added soap, and poured boiling water over the top. All of this to hide her disappointment. He'd done his job – Tobias had saved her life. Now he was doing all he could to rid himself of her.

~*~

As the sun set, Tobias seemed restless. He'd made his situation clear – he wanted her gone. Why, then, was he pacing the room? He'd already stated it was past his bedtime. Except he'd also told her he wasn't working in the morning. Instead, he would take her into town. Old habits die hard, she guessed.

It was then it hit her – Tobias only had one bed in the cottage. There was another room, he'd told her, but it was empty.

Not that he'd said so, but Emily wondered if that second room was for any future children. She shook herself mentally. It was not her business, and she needed to get it out of her mind.

"Emily," he finally said as he stopped pacing. "You take my bed tonight." His words were firm, but that did not mean she had to do what he said.

"No. I can sleep on the sofa comfortably. You can't." To prove her point, she lay down on the sofa and pulled the thick blanket up over herself.

Tobias muttered something but Emily wasn't sure what he'd said. She probably didn't want to know, either.

He stormed off into the bedroom and slammed the door closed. She had made him cross, there was no doubt. Emily had no intention of putting her rescuer out of his own bed. She would be fine here on the sofa.

Now all she had to do was convince herself the strange sounds she heard outside were completely normal.

Chapter Six

Tobias swore under his breath and hoped Emily didn't hear him. This is the reason he didn't open his heart to women. They would inevitably break it.

He was happy and comfortable here in his cottage. Sure, he felt lonely from time to time, but keeping busy remedied it. Most of the time, anyway.

Emily was already getting under his skin, and she hadn't been here all that long. He prayed the weather would hold, and he could deliver her to the sheriff's office in the morning. Then he could wipe his hands of her for good.

Except he already had feelings for her. Feelings he was fighting. He shook himself mentally. What he was feeling was not real. He felt sorry for the position she was in. It couldn't feel good to know someone was determined to dispose of you in the most heinous way. Tobias couldn't think of anything worse.

It got mighty cold out there in the forest, especially this time of the year. And that was when you were padded up with a thick coat, gloves, and scarf.

Emily was dumped in the snow, wearing a flimsy gown. If he'd found her even ten minutes later, he would have been delivering her body to the undertaker. If she hadn't been sobbing over her circumstances, he would not have discovered her for days.

What kind of monster did that to another person?

Tobias had repeatedly asked himself that question since the moment he found her unconscious in the snow. Dumped like a piece of garbage. A dog would be treated better than that.

The anger rose up through him, and Tobias knew he would never sleep. Besides, he wanted to stay in the sitting room for Emily's protection. If someone broke in, he would be right there. How did he do that if she was asleep in the other room?

Tobias knew he couldn't.

He sat on the side of the bed contemplating what to do next. Tobias was certain Emily thought the danger was over. He did not. If this gang got word she was still alive, they may come after her again. In fact, he was certain they would.

There was no other choice – Emily needed to sleep in his bed, and let Tobias do what he did best. Protect her.

~*~

Staring down into the face of an angel, he was now uncertain. Emily was sound asleep, and he was loathe to wake her. It left him with little choice – he carefully lifted her from the sofa and carried her to his bed. He peeled back the bedding, and carefully lay her down, then covered her. What Emily would say in the morning, he had no idea. But he knew he'd done the right thing.

Not that he expected anyone to come in through the bedroom window, but he left the bedroom door open, just in case. Then he reached for the rifle that sat above the fireplace. It had sat there for longer than Tobias could remember, and not once had he needed to take it down. He ensured it was loaded, then took his place on the sofa, facing the front door.

In case the rifle wasn't enough, his pistol sat firmly in its holster, fully loaded and ready if needed. Tobias took the threat seriously, even if Emily was convinced the danger was over.

The current situation brought back memories he would rather forget. His former life was something he would rather forget. It was the reason he'd left it all behind and isolated himself from society. Except now he found himself in the thick of it. Not that he blamed Emily for what happened, but he didn't need any of this.

Living his life as a recluse suited him. Cutting down trees for a living worked for Tobias. Folks knew where to find him if they needed timber to build with, or even for firewood. He rarely went to town, except to bolster his supplies.

Tomorrow he would take Emily to town, make a statement for the sheriff, and return back home. She would no longer be his responsibility. Why did the thought fill him with sadness? Tobias couldn't deny she had been a breath of fresh air, even with an attempt on her life.

Sitting upright, his back straight, on the sofa, kept him awake. He'd been awake since dawn, as he was most days. This was nothing new for him. How many times had he done this before? Far too many to remember. Despite the fact he tried to force it all out of his mind.

The fire was dying down. He stood, taking the rifle with him. Tobias would not let himself get caught off-guard. Throwing some logs on the fire would keep the cottage warm. Except it may also make him sleepy.

Coffee. That's what he needed. Tobias strolled into the kitchen and made himself a mug of strong, black coffee. It was then he heard it.

"No, Lonnie, please." Emily was begging for her life. How did the outlaw get in here without him hearing? The coffee forgotten, he ran to the bedroom, ready to kill the man on sight.

Except he wasn't there. No one was, except for Emily who was asleep.

She continued to scream in her sleep. Tobias had no doubt she was reliving her ordeal, but wasn't sure what to do about it. He sat on the side of the bed contemplating his next move.

With her arms flailing, Emily screamed again. It was breaking Tobias's heart. He shook himself mentally. This is exactly the reason he distanced himself from people. Keeping away meant he didn't have feelings for others. He wouldn't be expected to care for another person. Everyone in town knew he was a loner. Now he had to make sure Emily knew it too.

Coming to a decision, he gently shook her shoulder. "Emily," he whispered. "You need to wake up."

Her eyes fluttered open and she glanced up at him. Her mouth opened and he was certain she would scream. He did what anyone else would do – he covered her mouth with his hand. She struggled against him, leaving Tobias no choice. "It's me, Tobias," he said. "If you promise not to scream, I'll take my hand away."

Her eyes wide with terror, she nodded. He was true to his word – Tobias removed his hand. "You were having a nightmare," he told her. What he didn't say was if she continued to scream, and Lonnie was out there, he had no doubt she would be found. You could hear a pin drop in the forest at night. A scream would echo. If Lonnie was out there, he was almost guaranteed to hear it.

"I…I'm sorry," she whispered. Pulling the covers up to her neck for modesty, Tobias was certain, she sat up. "I can't get it out of my mind. His hands were around my throat." The last sentence had her eyes filling with tears.

"Nothing to be sorry about," Tobias said. "It was clear you were having a nightmare about what happened."

Emily was trying to fight back her tears. Tobias pulled her to his chest and let her cry. He didn't want to care about this stranger, but his heart was already telling him otherwise.

He couldn't wait for morning to come around so he could relieve himself of the responsibility.

Chapter Seven

Emily sat on the side of the bed with Tobias. After her incredibly realistic nightmare, she no longer wanted to sleep. The thought of closing her eyes was nightmare material, and once she closed them, Lonnie's hands around her throat played over and over again.

How could any man do such a heinous thing? It wasn't like it was a first for him – Emily was convinced Lonnie had killed before. He was completely calm as his hands tightened around her throat. He'd even smiled. A chill went through her entire being at the memory.

Holding back a sob, Emily shook her head. She couldn't fathom it. It took someone with a cold heart to do such a thing. She should have known – he'd snatched her from that stagecoach as though it was perfectly normal. As though it didn't matter he'd changed her life forever, that her family would be looking for her, worried about her.

Her heart was hollow. And her entire body shook at the realization. The fact she had survived was coincidental. If Tobias hadn't been in the vicinity of where Lonnie dumped her, she would not be alive now.

This time she couldn't stop herself from sobbing. Tobias's arm reached around her and he pulled her close. There was nothing he could do to stop her sobs, she had no control over them either, but his closeness and his caring made her feel worth something. Unlike Lonnie's actions.

When she was depleted, he lifted her chin with his fingers. His honey colored eyes bore into hers. He gazed at her for long moments, then swallowed hard. Tobias opened his mouth to speak, but paused momentarily. "None of this is your fault," he said firmly, then dropped his hand. "The kettle is boiled. I think tea is in order."

He stood then, and Emily did the same, forgetting about the flimsy nightshirt. Tobias turned his eyes away and reached for the thick robe. She quickly put it on, feeling exposed, but certain Tobias wouldn't use her vulnerability to his advantage. He wasn't like that.

Clinging to the rifle, he led her out to the kitchen, and sat her down at the table. He reached for two mugs, and filled one with tea, the other with strong black coffee. Despite the danger, Emily felt comfortable here. What she didn't feel was unsafe. Tobias was a good man, that much was clear from the moment she opened her eyes and found herself inside his home, despite her state of undress.

"Why do you live here alone?" she asked quietly. His eyes opened wide in amazement. Was it because she'd had the cheek to question him, or was there some other reason?

He opened his mouth to speak, then sipped his coffee instead. Tobias's eyes never left hers. "I prefer it that way," he finally told her. Only Emily didn't believe him. She wasn't sure why, but he didn't sound genuine. Or perhaps it was her imagination.

His cottage, at the edge of the forest, in the witching hour, left them both vulnerable. Especially with Emily in its midst. She had put Tobias in danger by her mere presence. He was right to rid himself of her in the morning. She was certain he would have done so sooner had the opportunity arisen. "I'm sorry," she whispered. "I'll be out of your hair in the morning."

His eyes bore into hers. "If this weather keeps up, we won't be going anywhere," he said gently. Emily knew that's what Lonnie had been counting on. She should have been covered by snow hours ago. His cruel plan should have worked, but thanks to Tobias, it didn't.

She lifted the mug to her lips and sipped slowly. "You're a good man, Tobias," she finally said, putting the mug to the table. "I'm sorry you were caught up in all this…" Emily thought for the right words, and finally it came to her. "This…this vile business."

His hand came across the table, and covered hers. She didn't pull it away. Having Tobias near gave her comfort, despite Emily knowing she shouldn't feel that way. Weather depending, he would rid himself of her first thing in the morning. The sheriff would deal with her in whatever way he felt appropriate. More than likely, after that, she would never see Tobias again.

The pounding on the door both startled and awoke Emily. Falling asleep on the sofa next to Tobias wasn't ideal, but she preferred that to having to sleep alone in the bedroom. Tobias had proven himself to be a good man, and had stayed awake the entire night to ensure her safety.

Rifle still in his hand, Tobias hurried to the door. "Who's there?" he called through the door.

The muffled voice replied. "Sheriff Gibson," he said.

Tobias stepped over to the window and carefully pulled back the curtains. Emily heard his sigh, even from so far away. "It's Sheriff Vern Gibson," he told her. Then unlocked the door and ushered the sheriff inside.

Emily watched their interaction with interest. Sheriff Gibson stared at the rifle in Tobias's hands. "What's this about then?" he asked harshly.

"You first," Tobias said. "What did you come here for?" His grip was still on the rifle, although he apparently knew this man. Tobias ushered him into the sitting room and indicated for him to sit down.

Sheriff Gibson brushed the snow from his thick jacket, and pulled off his gloves. He headed straight to the fire. "Come to warn you. There has been some sightings of a group of strangers in a wagon out this way." He glanced from Tobias to Emily. "Your turn," he said, his eyes now trained on Emily. The sheriff finally sat down, and continued to stare at her. It made Emily feel very uncomfortable.

"This is Emily Bishop. I believe she is the reason for those men being in this vicinity." Emily's heart thudded. She prayed the sheriff was truly trustworthy.

"Is that so," Sheriff Gibson asked. "I need more than that, Tobias. And you know it."

Still gripping the rifle tightly, Tobias relayed the story Emily did not want to have to repeat.

"That's one heck of a story, Miss Bishop. You never heard of the Jacobson gang?"

"Not before they snatched me," she said quietly. "Not that I had any choice."

Sheriff Gibson pulled off his hat and scratched his head. "They are vicious criminals. Lonnie is the worst of them all. He would never have let you walk away." As though he suddenly realized what he'd said, the sheriff apologized. "I'm sorry, Miss Bishop. That was rather insensitive of me."

Tobias moved closer to her, and put his arm around Emily's shoulders. "It certainly was, Vern," he said gruffly. "I'm sure Emily doesn't need to hear all the gritty details."

Emily swallowed down her emotions. The situation seemed to get worse by the day. "I need to leave here," she told the sheriff. "Staying puts Tobias in danger."

Sheriff Gibson laughed. "You didn't tell her?" he asked, turning to face Tobias. Then he shook his head. "Of course you didn't."

Tobias didn't say a word but shook his head ever so slightly. If she hadn't been staring at him, Emily would have missed it. Except she did see it, and now she needed answers. "What's going on?" she asked. "Tobias," she said firmly. "What are you hiding from me?"

Tobias continued to sit on the sofa, and still gripped the rifle like it was a lifeline. "In a past life, I was a bodyguard," he said, resignation in his voice.

It explained a lot. Especially why he was so determined to save her. Only in doing so, Tobias was also in danger. Emily wasn't sure how she would live with herself if something happened to him.

All because he'd tried to protect her.

Chapter Eight

Tobias had known Vern Gibson for a long time. Years. They first met when Tobias came to live here in Mountain Pass looking for a change in lifestyle. Merely thinking about that time in his life caused his heart to thud.

It was soon after his final job as a bodyguard. Most of his clients were high profile, and all needed to be babysat for one reason or another. The majority did what they were told – they were that scared. Except for his last. John Hanson laughed it off like a bad joke. He refused to follow instructions, and the inevitable happened. All that despite him being the one to contact Tobias.

Until now, Tobias had kept that time in his life way back in his memory. He didn't want to think about it ever again. Hanson had been a fool. He slipped outside when Tobias's back was turned. It only took one shot by his assassin.

Thinking about it again was not what he wanted. Tobias believed he'd finally rid himself of those memories. The nightmares had finally stopped a few years ago. Hard work and keeping himself busy was the only thing that helped.

Why did Vern have to bring it all to the surface again?

To be fair, seeing Emily unconscious in the snow had the same effect. He was taken right back to his days in Denver. It was all hustle and bustle back then. Tobias preferred the calm he had here. Although it was not the case right now, he had to admit.

He shook himself mentally. He had to forget Hanson, and concentrate on Emily. "What do you propose, Vern?" he asked carefully, knowing the sheriff would help him out.

"We need to get Miss Bishop into town. I'm not sure where we go from there, but she must be protected." He glanced at Emily, and Tobias saw her shudder. It was then Vern rubbed a hand across his unshaven chin. "You know, Tobias, you have compromised this little lady's respectability."

"Don't be absurd. I've done no such thing. What I have done, is save her life. If I hadn't brought her back here and kept her warm by the fire, she would be dead now." He glanced across at Emily. She shuddered, and he wasn't surprised.

Vern glanced about. His eyes focused on her clothes drying near the fire. "Are these your clothes, Miss Bishop?"

Her eyes shot straight to Tobias. Heat crept up her face, and Tobias dreaded the next words that would come out of Vern's mouth. "You need to marry her," Vern said briskly. "The preacher will sort it out for you."

"I…" Tobias was tongue-tied. He hadn't planned for this turn of events. He could, however, see where Vern was coming from. Doing the right thing had got him into a bucket load of trouble, and there was no way out.

"Get dressed, Miss Bishop. We're going to town," Vern ordered Emily. Her eyes flickered from Vern to Tobias. It was clear she was confused. "You get the buggy ready," Vern ordered Tobias, and he didn't argue. When Vern made up his mind about something, he was like a dog with a bone.

It seemed he and Emily would be married before the end of the day.

~*~

Wrapped in a thick blanket against the cold, Tobias helped Emily into the buggy. As he joined her, she leaned back and sighed. "What just happened?" she asked, her voice wavering. Are we being forced to marry? Did I understand correctly?"

"You did," Tobias answered. "It's not my choice either. I much prefer to live alone and not have to worry about anyone else." Emily grimaced. "No offense intended," he added quickly.

"What are we going to do? After my experience with Lonnie, I'm not exactly thrilled to be forced into marriage either."

Tobias frowned. Did that mean she didn't trust him? He was nothing like Lonnie Jacobson. Of all people, Emily should understand that. "I'm not sure we have much of a choice. After making our statement at the sheriff's office, we can talk with the preacher. He's a reasonable man." Tobias hoped that was true. It had been a while since he'd had much to do with the preacher. It wasn't that he didn't like going to church, he simply preferred his own company.

Emily reached for his hand, and a shiver went down his spine. Reacting to her touch was the last thing Tobias wanted. Except that wasn't true. Getting married to a complete stranger was the last thing he really wanted. But it seemed to be out of his hands. According to the sheriff at least. "I'm sorry to have put you in this situation," she whispered. "I didn't mean for this to happen. You saved my life, and now your entire life is being turned upside down."

She wasn't wrong. He had gone all this time, nearly four decades, without getting hitched. The worst of it all was he had no choice. According to Vern, anyways.

"Just so you know," Tobias said. "I'm no great catch. I cut down trees for a living. Mostly I cut them into firewood. Sometimes I dress timber for construction purposes. It makes me far from rich, but it's enough to be comfortable."

He could feel Emily's eyes burn into him. "You're a good man, Tobias. If they force this on us, I won't object."

Trying not to show his shock at her words, Tobias kept his eyes on the road ahead. The snow made it treacherous. It was slippery in parts, and therein lay the problem. Mulling Emily's words over in his head, he supposed marrying her wouldn't be too bad. Except he'd rather stay single.

No! He didn't want this, and neither her words nor her beauty would sway him. This proposed marriage was unwanted. At least on his part. He would do well to remember it.

"Won't be long and we'll arrive in town," he told her, his eyes not leaving the road ahead.

Emily didn't answer. He'd made his position clear. She appeared to be of a different mind. It was all he needed. As much as he might protest, they could still be forced into marriage. He always said it would be a cold day in hell before he married. It seemed that day had arrived.

Chapter Nine

Emily relayed her story to the sheriff, her heart pounding the entire time. Then it was Tobias's turn. He explained how he'd come to find her, and what happened after. Tobias paused and licked his lips, his eyes flickering her way. He explained how he'd had to completely undress her to save Emily's life. He'd then placed her near the fire wrapped in a thick blanket.

His words made her cringe, and she was certain it gave the sheriff even more ammunition to force them into marriage.

"I see," Vern said, as he wrote down the details. Without warning, he stood and stepped over to bulletin board on the other side of the room. He returned soon after, holding a wanted poster. "This the man?" he asked Emily.

She closed her eyes against the image in front of her, and let out a long breath. "That's Lonnie Jacobson," she declared. "His brothers were there too. They helped him." Tears rolled down her face as the reality of what they'd done hit. They had tried to murder her.

"I'm truly sorry, Miss Bishop," Sheriff Gibson said, and Emily believed him. "It can't be easy for you, knowing you were thrown away like a piece of trash."

"Vern!" Tobias said sternly. "That was totally unnecessary." The look on his face was ferocious. It surprised Emily that he stood up for her in this way. She did however, appreciate it. Tobias pulled out a handkerchief and wiped away her tears. Glancing at Vern, Emily was shocked to see a grin on the sheriff's face.

Was that because he now had more ammunition to force them into marriage? Or did he merely find Tobias's actions amusing? She would probably never know.

"You two need to find the preacher. Before you do though, a visit to Doc Billings is in order. As much as you did the right thing, Tobias, Miss Bishop needs the doc to check her over." Vern then ushered them out of his office.

"Vern's right, of course," Tobias said, and Emily held her breath waiting for him to continue. Did he mean about the marriage or the doctor's visit? "We should have visited Doc Billings before we talked to the sheriff." He shook his head then, which left Emily wondering what he was thinking now.

Arriving at the doctor's office, Tobias gave the man a brief description of what she had endured. Then he relegated Tobias to the waiting room, taking Emily into one of his examination rooms. "I need you to undress down to your undergarments, and climb up onto the exam table," he said in a manner that exuded his caring nature. His concern extended to the temperature of his hands. He waved them in front of the fire before touching her. Covering her with a crisp white sheet, Doc Billings ran his hands down her arms. He looked into her eyes, had Emily poke out her tongue, which she found most unladylike, and continued his thorough examination.

"Do you mind if I call Tobias in?" Doc Billings asked. "I'm certain he'll want to know the outcome."

Did she mind? Emily wasn't sure, but Tobias had saved her life. He didn't deserve to be kept in the dark, especially since it looked like they would soon become husband and wife. Emily finally nodded. She saw no harm in doing so.

Opening the door, the doctor waved Tobia in. "Miss Bishop is in good condition considering what she endured. She does have frostbite on her fingers, and a little on her toes."

Emily gasped. She hadn't noticed, but her mind had been in a whirl from the moment she woke up in Tobias's cabin.

Doc Billings put a hand to her shoulder. "It will disappear. You need to keep your extremities warm, and it will clear up. Thick socks and warm gloves, and a nice warm fire." He glanced across at Tobias. "You'll see to that, won't you Tobias?"

"Of course, Doc," Tobias said, but his eyes were on her, and not the kind and gentle doctor.

"You may get dressed now, Miss Bishop. You, Tobias, will leave the room. I'll come with you."

Both men hurried out of the room, leaving Emily alone to dress. It also left her alone with her thoughts. Next on the agenda was a visit to the preacher.

Emily was not looking forward to it.

Stepping outside the doctor's office, Emily shivered. Her thin cotton gown was no match to the cold weather, and she pulled the blanket around herself. Her only possessions were the clothes she stood up in. Out of the corner of her eye, she saw Tobias pull off his thick coat. He reached for the blanket and quickly draped his coat over her shoulders. "You didn't have to do that," she told him. "But I do appreciate it. Except now you'll be cold."

"Women feel the cold more than men. The blanket worked in the buggy, but you can't walk around with a blanket on your shoulders." He chuckled then, and Emily enjoyed the sound. With each waking moment she spent with this man, he surprised her a little more.

Despite him declaring he wanted to live alone, and didn't want to marry her, Emily had to wonder. He had found her and saved her life, then did everything possible to keep her alive. And now this. It seemed he was no longer trying to distance himself from her, and Emily wasn't complaining. Tobias made her feel safe and comforted.

Even though she knew she shouldn't.

Tobias lifted her up and carried her to the church. It would have been difficult to walk there. She had no shoes, and was wearing a pair of Tobias's thick socks. She was grateful for everything he'd done for her. It couldn't have been easy.

When they entered the church, Tobias gently put her to the floor. Emily's heart thudded. If she had to marry this man, she wanted to at least be presentable. She stared down at herself. Her gown was crumpled and grubby. She wore men's socks that were far bigger than respectable, and Tobias's oversized coat. Emily's heart felt hollow at the picture she portrayed.

No longer the gracious, independent woman she once was, Emily felt more like a street urchin. She couldn't marry anyone looking this way. Especially not Tobias who deserved far better.

Glancing up, she noticed the preacher coming toward them. She promptly sat down, hoping to cover her unseemly condition.

"Good morning, Preacher," Tobias said, his voice far from joyful. "Emily, may I introduce Preacher Samuel Chalmers."

The preacher looked her up and down, which didn't surprise Emily one bit. "Good morning to you both," he said, curiosity clear in his voice. He then sat himself on the wooden pew next to Emily. It made her feel curiously uncomfortable, given her state of dishevelment. "My dear girl," he said gently. "You look like you've been through hell and back."

Emily knew she shouldn't be, but was shocked at the preacher's words. "I really have," she said, staring down at her entwined hands as they sat on her lap.

His hand covered hers and he began to pray. By the time he finished, Emily felt as though a huge weight had been lifted from her shoulders.

"Preacher Chalmers," Tobias said, interrupting the calm that had engulfed her. "The sheriff says we have to get married."

The preacher studied Emily, and then Tobias. "Tell me why," he said, then listened carefully to Tobias as he relayed their story. Nodding his head, he agreed with the sheriff. "It might not be what either of you believe you want now, but I see the way you look at each other." He removed his hand from Emily's then stood. "Emily cannot marry like this. My wife can sort her out, but you'll need to go to the mercantile and outfit her. Wait here while I fetch Edna." He was gone before either of them could say a word.

Chapter Ten

By the time Edna Chalmers was done with her, Emily appeared to be a different person. Tobias couldn't believe the transformation. She'd had a hot bath, and while she did that, the preacher's wife took Tobias to the mercantile and helped him find clothes for Emily.

Her long hair had been fashioned in such a way she was unrecognizable. At least to Tobias. She wore boots that protected her feet, and meant she could now walk around unaided. He'd thought her beautiful before, but her beauty was now at a whole new level. It was all he could do not to gape.

Tobias and Preacher Chalmers had waited in the chapel, as they were ordered to do by the preacher's wife. Tobias was grateful for everything Mrs. Chalmers had done for Emily. Especially since he was only an occasional parishioner. And told the preacher so.

"My son, we do not judge. Emily needed help, and we are here to provide it." His words resonated with Tobias, and again he thanked the preacher for all he and his wife had done. The men stood as Emily entered the chapel once more. "You won't regret this marriage," the preacher whispered as they came closer.

"Hilda Williams, our organist will be here shortly. She will be your second witness." Mrs. Chalmers told them.

Tobias's breath caught him off guard. Now that he could see Emily up close, her beauty overwhelmed him. He knew she had a good heart, that much was clear. It was amazing what clean clothes and a hot bath had done. Not that she wasn't beautiful before, but now he got to see the woman beneath all that hurt and pain. Not to mention the worry that previously covered her face.

Of course she was still worried, but Tobias hoped her concerns were not as heavy as before.

"Tobias, you come down the front with me. Emily, rest your weary legs. Hilda should be here any minute."

Looking back down the aisle at his bride-to-be, Tobias couldn't understand why he'd ever doubted marrying Emily. It no longer bothered him, and he knew the preacher had put his mind at ease.

It wasn't long before Hilda Williams hurried through the chapel doors and took her place at the organ. The moment she began to play, Emily, with the help of the preacher's wife, slowly made her way down the aisle. His heart thudded. They were really doing this. In no time at all, they would be husband and wife, and Tobias world would never be the same again.

~*~

They walked arm in arm down the aisle toward the entrance to the chapel Mrs. Chalmers had helped Tobias choose more than one gown for Emily to marry in. She'd also helped select a full wardrobe of gowns, undergarments, stockings, socks, and nightgowns. Not to mention a thick coat, scarf and gloves, along with everything else she would need. He wished Emily could have chosen for herself, but the fewer people who saw her, the less to ask questions. With an entirely new name, she would be safer, but she still needed to make herself scarce.

Tobias would protect her with his life. It's what he did well. That was, before he became a lumberjack. He had fallen into it. He was a lost soul, his spirit and confidence broken over his dead client. Deep down he knew it wasn't his fault – the man refused to take orders from a *simple bodyguard*. At the time it made Tobias wonder why he'd been hired. His rates were not low. He effectively put his life on the line every time he agreed to protect someone.

Now he was doing it willingly. Even before Emily became his wife, he'd vowed to protect her, and he did. His biggest concern now was if Lonnie's gang came back to ensure she was dead. Surely they wouldn't be that stupid.

Except Tobias had first hand knowledge about the stupidity of killers. His heart thudded. "Emily, you wait here. I'll check outside to make sure it's safe. The expression on her face shattered his heart. Did she think by marrying him the danger would simply disappear? She was wrong. It could be months before they were certain it was safe again.

Tobias opened the heavy door and stepped outside. Hand hovering above his holster, he was ready for anything. Glancing about, he didn't see anything or anyone untoward, and breathed a huge sigh of relief. As he turned to go back inside, he felt eyes burning into his back.

Spinning around, Tobias was relieved to discover it was Sheriff Gibson. The man almost ran toward him, the question already on his lips. "What did the preacher say?" he asked when he was close enough he didn't need to shout.

"It's done," Tobias told him firmly, then went back inside without another word.

He should have realized the sheriff would follow him in. He would want proof they'd married, not that it was his business.

"Preacher, Mrs. Chalmers," Vern Gibson said. "Hilda, I didn't see you there."

Samuel Chalmers stepped forward and greeted the sheriff. "Welcome, Vern. It's been a while." He changed the subject abruptly. "What are you doing to protect this young lady, Vern? She's a sitting duck."

Heat traveled up Vern's neck. "The danger is over," he said, sounding unsure of himself.

Tobias didn't believe that. "Until the entire Jacobson gang are behind bars, we can't be sure of anything." He heard his wife gasp. It wasn't his intention to upset or worry her, but to have Vern take action. "The least you should do is contact the marshals. They've been after this gang for years, and we both know it."

"Why did Lonnie choose me?" Emily asked, her voice full of emotion. "I was minding my own business when they attacked." She wiped at her eyes, then added, "He held a gun at my head and…threatened to shoot if I didn't go with him. As if that wasn't enough, he then tried to murder me."

"Oh, you poor thing," Edna Chalmers said, and wrapped Emily in her arms. "Vern you arrange for those marshals. Emily needs to be safe." She stood back a little and stared into Emily's eyes. "We need to know she is safe."

Tobias could see Vern was uncomfortable being ordered about. Perhaps it would move him to action. Tobias certainly hoped it would. "Anything I can do to help, Sheriff?" he asked, but Vern glared at him, so he stepped back.

"I'll contact the marshals and hopefully get them here," the sheriff announced, then turned on his heel and left the building without another word.

"I'm certain the marshals will come," Tobias said. What he didn't say was he didn't feel confident enough to protect Emily alone. Not if the entire gang turned up on his doorstep. If that happened, Tobias and his new bride didn't stand a chance.

Chapter Eleven

Emily wasn't stupid. She'd already worked out she was a sitting duck. If Sheriff Gibson was unable to convince the marshals to help out, not only would Lonnie and his brothers kill her, they would kill Tobias as well.

That didn't sit well with Emily. He was an innocent victim in all of this. Truth be told, she was too. How many times had Lonnie done this before? Did he snatch random women often? He had quickly tired of her, and it immediately put her in Lonnie's firing line.

Had she died out there in the snow, Tobias would not be in imminent danger. He was a good man and didn't deserve the trouble she'd caused him. That went for the township of Mountain Pass, as well. Those people were all innocent, and may be targeted for simply being in the vicinity of Emily.

Her heart shattered at the thought.

She had no means to leave, but even if she did, Lonnie could still slaughter everyone here. Her heart was broken, and her mind in a whirl.

Tobias gazed into her face. "Everything will work out," he said softly. It was almost as though he could read her mind. Of course that wasn't true. He understood what she wanted to hear. Knew what to say to make her feel better. Only it didn't. Emily had put him in an untenable position.

Confessing he was a bodyguard didn't come easy for Tobias. Despite not doing that job for some years, he had done his best to protect her. Lonnie didn't show, but that wasn't the point. Tobias was willing to protect Emily from her would-be killer. "You could be wrong," she whispered, and he frowned.

"Lonnie would be a fool to return here," he said quietly but firmly. "There's only one reason he would come back." She watched him flinch once the words were out.

"To make sure I was dead," Emily said, holding back her emotions. "When he discovers I am alive and well…"

"It won't get to that point," Tobias said, interrupting her. "The marshals have been after that gang for years. They will come here as a matter of urgency. You mark my words."

His arm slipped around her shoulders, and Emily felt strangely comforted. All this talk of Lonnie and death had her on the cusp of breaking down. Tobias holding her like this meant the world.

As though he knew what she was thinking, he pulled her into a bear hug, and held her close. Her head resting on her chest, Emily could hear his heart beat. Instead of slow and steady, it was racing. Much like her own. He leaned in and kissed her forehead. Then whispered in her ear. "I will protect you. I don't believe Lonnie will return." His words were firm. Not only did he want Emily to believe him, but it was almost as though he was trying to convince himself.

She could stand there and argue, or Emily could stay where she was and enjoy his nearness. Arguing was not in her nature, so instead, she stayed wrapped in the arms of the man who had nominated himself her defender.

No words were spoken as they left Mountain Pass. Once outside of town, Emily felt she owed Tobias a lot. "I can leave," she said. "Take me back to town and I'll get the next stagecoach out. That way you won't have to worry about me."

"Whoa," he called to the horses, and they came to a halt. Tobias turned to her. "What sort of man do you think I am?" he demanded, despite keeping his voice low. "You are my wife, and I will look out for you." He leaned in and hugged Emily, his warm breath fanning her cheek.

"I should have refused to marry you. That way you wouldn't feel obliged to care for me." She turned her face away, not wanting to see the expression on his face. It may only confirm what she'd been thinking. Being forced to marry her under duress left him bitter.

Tobias didn't say anything for what seemed an eternity but was probably only thirty seconds. He lifted her chin to face him again. "I don't feel obligated. I admit, I didn't want to marry, but it wasn't personal. Since I did have to, I'm glad it was to you."

It brought a smile to her lips, and his lips curled too. "We need to get back. You are too vulnerable out here." He leaned in and brushed his lips across hers, then quickly turned back to the horses. Tobias acted as though his kiss hadn't sent a tingle down her spine. Or left an indelible mark on her lips.

Emily knew things would never be the same between them. Except Tobias hadn't said their marriage would be a real one. He also hadn't told her it was a marriage of convenience. She supposed the circumstances were different to the norm. Difficult. For both of them. Emily would wait and see how things panned out, but she already had feelings for Tobias. She doubted he felt the same.

Startled awake, Emily wasn't sure where she was. "Wake up, sleepyhead. We're home." Tobias voice came through loud and clear. Her head rested on his shoulder. Emily wasn't sure how he'd feel about that. When she glanced at him, Tobias seemed amused, not annoyed at all. He climbed down from the buggy, and quickly went to her side. His hands outstretched, he helped Emily down.

Unlocking the door, he deftly picked her up and carried Emily across the threshold. "What…?" she asked, confused.

"Can't have my bride walk inside unaided. Besides, it's tradition," Tobias told her.

For two people who were forced into an unwanted and unwelcome marriage, they both seemed happy enough. Emily wondered if that might change as the days progressed.

Tobias gently put her to the floor, then reached for her hand. "I have to fix up the horses. Before I do that though, I need to check it's safe for you in here." Taking her with him, Tobias went from room to room ensuring no one lurked behind doors, in closets, under the bed, or hidden anywhere else. When he was done, he led Emily to the sitting room and indicated for her to sit. "Wait here. I'll lock this door behind me," he said gently. He kissed her forehead, then disappeared out the door.

Despite what he'd said, she pushed the curtain aside and watched as he led the horses into the large barn. Tobias was a good person. He didn't have to marry her, and he didn't have to protect her. It would have been far easier if the marshals took her into custody and protected her. Why Emily didn't think of that when the sheriff practically forced them together, she didn't know.

She knew it wasn't too late to get an annulment and let the marshals look after her. That way Tobias wouldn't be in danger, and he could go back to his normal, peaceful life. The one that he preferred.

Chapter Twelve

Tobias reluctantly left Emily waiting in the house. It tore at his heart to leave her there alone, but he had to tend to the horses. They needed brushing down and feeding. His horses were important and had to be properly cared for.

As he led them away from the cottage, he felt Emily's eyes burn into his back. So much for being discreet. It took all his effort not to turn around and scowl at her. If it wasn't for the potential of prying eyes, he probably would have done just that. Tobias had already scanned the area to ensure they were alone. Just because they hadn't got into the cottage didn't mean Lonnie and his gang were not around.

More than likely they were, Tobias was certain. If not now, then sometime down the track. He'd put himself in Lonnie's shoes, and knew he would do the same. It was pure luck he was in the right place at the right time, otherwise it would have been certain death for Emily. *His wife.*

It took a lot of effort to get used to having a wife. Being a husband. He'd never contemplated it as a bodyguard, since the life was not conducive to marriage. When he moved out here, Tobias decided no woman would be happy living this far from town. He still believed it was true.

It would be interesting to see how long it took Emily. Would she leave once the danger was over? He was willing to bet she would only last a few weeks at most. She was a city girl. From what he understood, she was born and bred in Helena. Mountain Pass was but a blink of the eye in comparison.

As he unhitched the buggy from the horses, he placed each one in their stalls. He brushed them down and fed them. It was then it hit him. Tobias hadn't checked the barn. His own stupidity could have got him killed. Not to mention Emily. She had cheated death once. Twice would be a miracle.

He snatched the rifle from under the seat of the buggy, while reassuring himself of the Colt that sat in his holster. He needed to be ready for anything. And that included the possibility of gang members hiding in his barn.

The hairs on the back of his neck stood up, and a shiver went down his spine. Someone was here. Whether that was the Jacobson gang, he couldn't be sure. What Tobias did know was there was an intruder in his barn.

Standing outside each stall, he threw the doors back, one by one. Each one was clear. The only other possible hiding place was the loft. It wasn't huge, but four men could easily hide there, but no more. Not without being incredibly uncomfortable.

He slowly climbed the ladder, rifle still firmly in his hands. His heart thudded and he was on high alert. It reminded Tobias exactly why he'd walked away from his work as a bodyguard. It wasn't a good life, especially for a man approaching the wrong side of forty.

Lifting his head slowly to peer into the loft, Tobias saw nothing. There was no one here. Being thorough as he knew he needed to be, Tobias climbed up onto the loft. He pushed the hay around with his foot, but suddenly stopped.

The noise he'd heard had him on alert once more. The hissing became louder as he moved deeper into the loft. It was darker back here, but he should still see anyone who tried to hide there with the help of the lantern he kept at the top of the ladder. "Show yourself," he demanded as he lit the lantern. Instead of an answer, the hissing began again. It made him even more curious.

If Lonnie were here, Tobias wouldn't be standing now. What he was dealing with, he couldn't begin to fathom. This area had all sorts of wild critters. They would be looking for a warm place to get out of the cold and the snow.

A pair of eyes lit up from the beam of the lantern. Tobias sighed with relief. He had a barn cat. It was years since the loft was blessed with cats. As he moved closer, the hissing began again. This barn cat had a litter of kittens, which she was feeding. She was warning him to stay away from her babies.

Tobias was sure Emily would love to see this beautiful sight. Except it might put her in danger. Perhaps tomorrow when there was more light, he might bring her up here. Mother cat needed nurturing if she was to feed her babies. Tobias shook himself mentally. He had more important things to think about than cats. If he told Emily she would definitely want to check them out for herself.

He backed away, then climbed down the ladder. Scanning the area again, and checking the stalls once more, to ensure he was still alone, then headed back to the horses. Tobias had always found brushing his horses therapeutic, and often spent long hours brushing them. He was on edge, and needed to get back to Emily.

He told himself it was because he needed to protect her. His mind told him one thing, but his heart told him something entirely different.

~*~

It had taken longer than he'd hoped to finish up in the barn. Mother cat was on his mind, along with Emily. He worried about his horses. If the Jacobson gang did turn up at the cottage, would they target his horses? Kill them, or steal them? Either way wasn't palatable.

Tobias never locked the barn, but today he did exactly that. The more difficult he made it for the outlaws, the better. As he closed the padlock, he breathed a sigh of relief. The rifle was still firmly in his hand, and he was ready to use it. Emily's box of clothes was at his feet. As he leaned down to pick it up, Tobias glanced about again. His skills were not going to waste. He knew exactly what needed to be done to protect his wife, and he would do it.

Still, if a marshal or two turned up, he would feel far more comfortable. He had to sleep sometime, and doing so could mean those despicable men got to Emily. It was the last thing he wanted.

The most time Tobias knew he could stay awake was close to forty-eight hours. Except that was years ago. He'd not had to do that since his last protection job. It was already over a day since he had closed his eyes, and even then, he was still awake.

He struggled through the snow, which was far heavier now, and headed for the front door. He snatched up some logs for the fire before he entered the cottage. As he arrived, the door opened. Emily stood smiling at him. Tobias's heart fluttered. Since when did Emily cause this reaction?

What he needed to do was treat her like a client. After all, that's what she was. All he had to do now was tell himself that. If he hadn't married her, it would be easy. That's exactly what he was doing until the sheriff had come along and twisted everything out of proportion.

"I told you to stay inside," he growled as she opened the door wider.

Her smile turned to a frown, and Emily stormed off into the kitchen. "I knew it was you," she said, her back to him. "I saw through the window."

Another thing she shouldn't be doing.

Glancing across, Tobias saw she'd lit the fire. He closed the door and locked it. He placed her new clothes on the low table in the sitting room, then followed her into the kitchen. The warmth from the cookstove hit him in the face, and he realized she'd lit that too. At least she must have refilled it with wood. He always kept it going.

She stood at the sink, staring out the kitchen window. The curtains there were flimsy – she really shouldn't be standing there. It felt as though she was exposed in every direction. Except Emily didn't seem worried. She knew Lonnie and his brothers better than anyone. Was she right? Would they stay away?

Tobias was conflicted. He was almost certain the Jacobson gang would not stay away. Lonnie needed to know there were no witnesses to his murderous intent. Tobias had dealt with far too many criminals and outlaws over his years as a bodyguard. They inevitably thought they could outsmart the law. If they thought they'd left evidence behind, they would go back and try to remove it. In this case, Emily's body.

Except she was here, and not where they dumped her. It broke his heart they'd treated her like a piece of trash. Like something that mattered to no one.

She mattered to him. Emily was a real live person and deserved far better. He had to ensure she was treated like the woman she was.

Chapter Thirteen

Emily was furious. She'd seen Tobias had his arms full, and wanted to help. She was careful not to be seen from outside, both when she peered around the curtains, and when she opened the door. And all he could do was admonish her for it. For helping him?

She stood at the sink, arms crossed in front of her. Emily stared out into the grassy area in front of her. It was far too open here. Plenty of ways for Lonnie to get in if he wanted. As she continued to stare, Emily noticed the small vegetable patch. It was overrun with weeds, and needed a loving hand to get it back on track.

Emily supposed that was out of the question too.

While Tobias had been outside, she did a bit of checking. The pantry was almost full, and she had plenty to work with for meals. It wasn't like Tobias couldn't cook – the stew he'd made yesterday was very tasty, but Emily had no idea what else he knew how to cook. There was a plentiful supply of eggs due to the handful of chickens he had running around. She guessed he wouldn't let her collect eggs either.

Sighing, she wondered what she could do to help. Even doing laundry was out of the question, all that was left for her was cleaning house and cooking. She wasn't a housekeeper! Instead of feeling better, have calmness come over her, it was the opposite. Anger built up inside her, until she was on the verge of an explosion.

As if he sensed the way she was feeling, Tobias came up behind her. His arms held her close. "It's for your own safety," he whispered, and Emily knew he was right. Against her wishes, she leaned into him, her back against his chest.

"I am bored," she said quietly, her anger beginning to dissipate. "I hope you like cake, and other sweet things. That's probably how I will spend my days." There was a hint of sarcasm in her voice, which she hadn't intended. She wasn't the best cook, but she could make do.

He leaned down and whispered in her ear. "I love cake," then chuckled. It soon turned into a belly laugh. Tobias had an infectious laugh, and soon Emily joined him, despite her anger of only minutes ago.

Tobias was full of surprises. Those three small words lifted her spirits far higher than she expected possible under the circumstances. "I have something to tell you," he said when they both calmed down. Emily turned to face him. His bland expression meant she couldn't tell if it was something serious.

The truth was, there was little going on at the moment that would make her cheerful. That only meant bad news. "Do I need to sit down for this?" she asked, her heart pounding. Emily was truly afraid of what he might say.

His lips curled and his eyes became bright. "I found something in the loft. A barn cat with a litter of kittens."

Dread turned into happiness, and Emily couldn't believe what she was hearing. "Is it true or are you making it up?" She hoped it was true – they both needed good news.

Tobias pulled her closer and wrapped Emily in his arms. "It is true, I promise. If it's safe, perhaps we'll go up into the loft tomorrow, but not for long." Her joyfulness turned to sorrow. She wanted to go immediately, but had to trust Tobias's instincts. If he wanted her to wait until tomorrow, that's what she would do. Mother cat needs milk," he said. "That's settled then. Now what did you say about cake?"

Emily playfully slapped his arm. If she had to be in isolation with someone, she was glad it was Tobias.

~*~

Sleep had been fitful. It was their wedding night, and they shared the one bed, but Tobias was a gentleman. Fully dressed, he held her close until she fell asleep. He did not attempt anything more. They were still on high alert in case Lonnie came looking for her. Tobias told her, despite being in bed, and perhaps even sleeping, he would protect her from any attack.

Emily had to believe him. Her husband was an experienced bodyguard, and promised he would defend her until the bitter end. She didn't want him to die trying to save her. He was the innocent party in all of this.

Of course, Emily was innocent too, however, if not for her, Tobias would not be in danger. The very thought of losing him shattered her. Now that she knew how brutal Lonnie could be, Emily knew he would not make it a quick, clean death. It seemed he wanted his victims to linger. To feel pain as they slipped away.

The very thought of it brought tears to her eyes. Tobias pulled her a little closer. "What's wrong?" he asked. How he knew she was upset, Emily had no idea.

"Nothing," she said, trying to rally, but he didn't believe her.

He leaned forward and kissed her cheek. Wiping her tears away, he rolled Emily to face him. "We will get him, have no fear. Jacobson and his brothers will not be around much longer. They will pay for what they did to you." He sounded angry, and Emily could understand why. Lonnie and his brothers had completely changed Tobias's life.

Because he'd saved her, he was given no choice but to marry her. It was not a choice Tobias had made for himself.

The moonlight slipped into the room through the thin curtains. If she survived this ordeal, Emily would make new curtains. The window coverings needed to actually hide what was inside the room.

Her mind was all over the place, and she knew it. Glancing up at Tobias, the moonlight sent shadows across his face. The bed had streaks of light and shadow. She reached up and stroked his cheek. Tobias caught her hand and brought it to his lips. He kissed her hand oh so lightly, and a shiver went down Emily's spine.

She gasped at the shadow that suddenly appeared. "He's…" She swallowed hard. "He's here," she whispered, and pointed to the silhouette that lay across the bed.

Tobias was out of bed in a flash. He grabbed the rifle he'd left on the floor beside the bed, and the handgun that lay under his pillow. Emily's heart pounded. If she hadn't been laying down, she was certain she would have fainted from the shock she received.

Forcing herself to focus, Emily climbed out of bed and pulled on her robe. She followed Tobias into the kitchen and lit the lantern at his request. He whispered for her to open the door. She couldn't have been more shocked. Reluctantly, Emily did as she was told.

She was shocked when he suddenly lay down his firearms.

Chapter Fourteen

Tobias was certain this was the end. As Emily pulled the door fully open at his request, his heart pounded. Gun in hand, the stranger standing in the doorway was big and strong. And determined.

"Don't shoot," the stranger said urgently. "Marshal Peter Dodson, here to protect you."

Tobias wasn't prepared to believe the man on his word, but the badge he held was all the proof he needed. "Marshal, it is good to see you. Are you alone?" Worry filled him. Two were better than Tobias alone, but not if they went up against the entire Jacobson gang.

Marshal Dodson chuckled. "Are you kidding? We've been after this gang for years. They are elusive, that's for sure." He shrugged off his heavy jacket and pulled off his hat. He stomped, shaking the snow from his boots, then ran his fingers through his hair. "The others are checking the barn, and the area, and will be inside shortly. Miss Bishop, where will I find her?" he asked as he glanced about.

Tobias nodded for Emily to show herself. "It's Mrs. Harrison," she said as she faced the marshal.

"Of course, apologies Mrs. Harrison. You are one of the few people to survive the Jacobson gang. They are brutal, as you have discovered." He turned and closed the door behind him. "You were not their first victim. From what we can tell, all Lonnie's kidnap victims were eliminated once he tired of them. That is conjecture, as no other witnesses survived. We're here to ensure you are safe."

Tobias put an arm around his wife. All color had drained from her face. Would she faint? Instead of allowing that to happen, he led her to a chair, then turned to the marshal. "Take a seat, Marshal Dodson. Coffee?" He didn't wait for an answer. Instead, Tobias headed to the kitchen and pulled down some mugs. With no idea of how many marshals were here, he pulled down four mugs. Dodson would have at least one partner, he was certain. At least he hoped he did.

"That sounds good, thanks," Dodson called. Then his voice became muffled. Tobias was certain he was questioning Emily, and didn't want to leave her alone. He hurried back into the sitting room.

"It will take a few minutes for the kettle to boil," he said. It was an outright lie, but he wanted to ensure his wife was not being badgered by this man they didn't know.

He sat down and Dodson spoke, his gaze on Tobias. "I was just telling your wife, there are four of us. The others should be in shortly. I hope that's alright with you."

Relief overcame Tobias. It meant they had the man power to subdue the Jacobsons. He glanced at Emily. She seemed equally relieved. Color was back in her face, and he was certain this new information had caused it. "I'm feeling better now," she said firmly. "I'll make the coffee." Not giving him any choice, she hurried into the kitchen.

Tobias followed. He didn't want her left alone for even a few minutes. If four marshals were here, they knew the danger was high. He hoped Emily hadn't come to the same conclusion. She was already terrified of what Lonnie would do to her if he found her alive and well. He was not the sort of man to accept failure.

If he suspected she was alive, he would come looking. Tobias's was the only cottage at the edge of the forest. In fact, it was the only building for miles around. He expected nothing less than Lonnie coming to the conclusion she was here.

The very thought shattered his heart. Not for himself, but for Emily. She'd done nothing wrong. Except in Lonnie's eyes, not dying out there would be her defying him. He wouldn't let it pass. He couldn't afford to. Not only could she testify against him, but his reputation as a hardened criminal and killer would be destroyed.

The knock on the door brought him back to the present. Tobias knew better than to pre-empt the way things would go, but this time it was personal. Dodson stood and hurried to the door. "All clear," the man said. Dodson ushered him inside. Two more marshals followed.

"Take a seat gentlemen," Tobias said. "Coffee is on the way."

The three marshals relieved themselves of the snow on their hats and coats, and stomped until their boots were snow-free. Peter Dodson introduced them as Dillion Huggins, Ethan Mercer, and Ben Delany. He insisted they were addressed by their Christian names. Tobias said they should do the same to Emily and himself.

The moment the introductions were over, Emily excused herself to prepare coffee. No one objected. Tobias guided them into the kitchen where Emily placed the drinks on the kitchen table, along with a plate of pound cake.

"This will go down a treat," Peter Dodson said. "It's been a long day getting here," he added.

Ben Delany glanced up and momentarily stopped drinking the hot liquid in front of him. "This is mighty good cake, Emily," he said, then went back to his coffee.

Tobias had to agree. Not that she'd had much time to bake, but Emily had done so soon after they'd come home. He knew very little about her, but one thing he did know, she was an excellent cook. Thankfully they had plenty of supplies, and he hoped his wife could make something out of whatever was available. Feeding six mouths instead of two was a big ask. He hoped Emily was up for it.

She stood looking down at their guests, as though she was taking it all in. "Have you men eaten today?" she asked.

Peter Dodson glanced up at her. "Don't worry about us, Mrs… er, Emily. We've survived on less."

Tobias noticed the determined look in her eyes, and knew instinctively what would happen next. She headed to the bedroom, and was back soon afterwards. This time she was fully dressed and ready for action. The determination on her face told him far more about his wife than he knew already.

She had been through so much, but that one action told him a lot about her strength of character. Everything she'd endured since Tobias found her alone in the snow had told him so much about her. Emily's actions spoke far louder than words. "What do you need me to do?" he asked, already predicting the answer.

"Sit down and drink your coffee. I've got this," she said firmly.

The four marshals turned to him and grinned. At least they understood what they were up against.

Chapter Fifteen

Emily hurried into the pantry. She'd had a cursory glance earlier, but had only taken note of what she needed for supper. This time she took in the entire inventory available to her. What she needed was something quick and easy to make. This hour of the night demanded it.

She snatched up flour and eggs, then reached into the icebox for milk and butter. Carrying them back into the kitchen, she decided to fry some potatoes and onions to make the meal more substantial.

It was then Emily realized she should have taken up Tobias offer to help. Too late now. She could come back a second time, or send him to get the necessary ingredients.

Placing everything on the kitchen counter, Emily glanced across at the five men sitting at the table. They appeared deep in conversation, their voices low. It appeared serious, and she didn't want to disturb them. She returned to the pantry, quickly finding the remaining ingredients. It had been a while since she'd cooked for this many. Emily hoped she made enough to go around.

She'd seen a large frying pan earlier, and pulled it out of the cupboard. Before anything else, she needed to peel and dice the vegetables and get those cooking. Then, and only then, could she begin to prepare the pancakes.

Peeling potatoes proved to be therapeutic. It had forced her to slow down, even if only for a while. The frying pan was heating up while she prepared the vegetables, which were almost ready. Throwing them on the stove, she wondered again, would it be enough. Now she had slowed down, Emily knew no matter how much or what she served up, these men would appreciate food in their bellies.

The sizzling pan in the background drowned out the muffled words of the five men. No doubt they were talking strategies. Emily was happy to leave them to it. They had their area of expertise, and she had hers. After throwing the vegetables into the hot pan, she gave them a good stir, then began work on the pancake mix. Despite eating earlier, Emily was certain Tobias would be happy to accept more. The thought made her chuckle. Until she remembered the last time she'd made this meal – it was for Lonnie and his brothers, only days before they tried to kill her.

~*~

There was nothing more satisfying, at least to Emily, to watch men enjoying a meal she'd prepared. Coffee seemed to be a staple for them, and she kept their mugs filled. There was leftover apple pie from the meal she and Tobias had shared earlier, so Emily knew they wouldn't go hungry.

Sleeping arrangements were another thing altogether. There was a spare room, but no spare bed. It was simply an empty space. The cottage was built long before Tobias bought the place, and was built for a small family.

Knowing the men would come to some sort of arrangement themselves, Emily left her words unsaid. She would concentrate on keeping them happy with good food, and Tobias could deal with the rest.

"Thank you for a delicious meal," Marshal Dodson said. He seemed to be speaking on behalf of them all.

"You are welcome," Emily said. "I am about to dish up apple pie." She turned her back to do exactly that before he had a chance to say any more. It was a pity it wasn't piping hot, because pie was at its best then.

Handing out the desserts, Emily felt she had at least contributed something. It was difficult sitting back and doing little to help. Tobias reached for her hand as she turned away to collect more desserts to distribute.

He seemed to be enjoying a second dinner, as she was sure he would. "You are an excellent cook," Tobias said, a glint in his eye. The marshals all glanced up and grinned.

There was a collective murmur about her cooking skills. Emily was limited in what she knew how to cook, but was willing to learn.

Pouring herself a mug of tea, Emily excused herself and headed to the sitting room. The marshals clearly wanted to talk to Tobias. Whether that was strategies, or updating him on what little was known about Lonnie and his brothers, she didn't know.

The fewer times she heard his name, the better. Simply thinking about her would-be killers and what they'd done to her, send shivers down her spine. How any man could do such a thing and walk away with a clear conscious, Emily didn't know.

What she did know, was she'd never be the same again.

The warmth of the fire was comforting. Emily sipped her tea, and let it slide down her throat. The mug heated her hands, and the smooth liquid brought her comfort. The moment the men stopped talking amongst themselves, she would return to the kitchen and clean up the mess.

She was glad they hadn't included her in their discussions. The less she knew about her abductors, the better. Until that moment he'd tried to choke her, Emily thought she was relatively safe. At least while she followed Lonnie's orders. As the days went on, she could see his impatience with her. If she'd been younger, he might have kept her longer. It became clear relatively quickly he preferred a younger woman.

And Emily was far from that.

Emily shook her head, trying to chase away the memories. Her heart pounded, and Emily knew she had to get it out of her mind. Instead, the memory of her body turning to ice as she lay in the cold and the snow returned. How Lonnie, admittedly a hardened criminal, could dump her like that, Emily would never know.

The very thought of it broke her heart. She lay back in the comfortable chair, and let herself be warmed by the fire. The same fire that saved her from certain death. But not without the help of Tobias Harrison.

He was her rescuer, her redeemer. The complete opposite of Lonnie, and yet, she had put his life in danger. This time it felt as though her heart shattered into a million pieces.

Chapter Sixteen

The five men headed into the sitting room with their refilled coffee mugs. Despite the warmth from the cookstove, it was a little chilly in there, as it tended to be late at night. The warmth of the fire in the sitting room was far greater. No doubt Emily was enjoying it.

Tobias was happy with the strategies the marshals had worked out – two men on, two off. There had been no updates on Lonnie Jacobson or his brothers. They seemed to have disappeared into oblivion. It was nothing new. After each murder, they'd done the same thing.

They went on their violent sprees on a regular basis. At least once a month, but often far more. They spared no one. If someone got in their way, they were eliminated. The life of others meant nothing to them. What they'd done to Emily proved that point.

His heart pounded. Tobias glanced across to where he knew his wife would be sitting. She was sound asleep. His hope was her nightmares were gone, but knew it was an impossible ask. How Emily would ever recover from her ordeal, he didn't know. What he knew was he'd be right there by her side, helping her through it.

Turning to the others, he put a finger to his lips, then lifted Emily into his arms. Carrying her into the bedroom, he glanced down into her face. Even in sleep, her worry was clearly evident. If it was the last thing he ever did, he would ensure Lonnie Jacobson would never get near to Emily ever again.

If that meant he had to kill the man to do it, so be it.

He placed Emily in the bed and pulled the covers over her. Tobias stared down into her face. She was beautiful, not only on the outside, but the inside as well. Her biggest fault was her trust in people. Tobias knew from experience even the most violent of criminals could earn the trust of those around them.

Someone like Emily trusted easily. It often got them killed. His heart pounded. His precious wife almost died.

As he straightened, Tobias realized his stance had changed. He'd been forced into marriage with Emily, and was resentful. Not toward her, but the sheriff. But now, the pair had spent a lot of time together, and he'd gotten to know her well. Could he be falling in love with his wife? Even after such a short time?

Tobias shook his head trying to clear his mind. He was not one for frivolities. He was not interested in love or women. Nor did he have an interest in all the things that went along with them.

Except Emily was different. He sat on the edge of the bed. His head in his hands, Tobias sat quietly for a few minutes, simply contemplating his feelings. There was no conclusion forthcoming, so he stood, and glanced down at his wife again.

A shadow came over her. When he glanced up, he saw nothing but the moon.

His hands gripped the rifle he'd held earlier as he sat on the chair in the bedroom. Emily was still sound asleep. Tobias wouldn't wake her unless it was completely necessary. Three of the four marshals were out scouring the area, the fourth stayed behind and was in the sitting room.

Tobias's heart pounded. Was Lonnie Jacobson here? Why had he come back so quickly? He wondered if the man had stayed in town and seen Emily with him. If *he* had put her in danger. If *he* had signed her death warrant.

It was enough to shatter his heart.

He heard voices. Muffled, but they were there. Outside. In the cold night air. His heart pounded as he waited. The few minutes he waited seemed like hours.

Finally, to his great relief, Marshal Ben Delaney stood at the bedroom door. "It's all clear," he whispered. Moments later he was gone.

Tobias glanced at the window with its thin coverings. He'd never worried about them before. No one came out here at night. Nor did they come in the early hours of the morning. Even if they did, people didn't glance through his bedroom window.

Except now he had a wife. A wife who was in extreme danger. He strode over to the robe and pulled open a drawer. He had sheets and blankets, pillowcases, along with clothes he no longer wore. Tobias found nothing suitable to block staring eyes.

Until his own eyes landed on his robe. The one he'd given Emily to wear. The same one that was at least two sizes too big for her. It was thick, and it was large. It would protect her from prying eyes, now that she had her own robe.

It wasn't easy, but he managed to hang the robe over the window. He was flummoxed to begin with, but then removed the current flimsy covering, and threaded the arms of the robe through the curtain rod. It wasn't the prettiest of coverings, but it did the job at hand.

Emily moaned in her sleep, then rolled over to face him. Her eyes opened wide, then closed again. A smile came to her face, but quickly went.

If he had the luxury of time, Tobias would lay down beside her. Except he needed to know what was going on. What the marshals had found, if anything. It was obvious the Jacobson's were not found. They would have told him that much.

Assured Emily was asleep again, he pulled the covers up around her shoulders, and gently kissed her cheek. This time she didn't move. She was once again in a deep sleep.

It was safe for Tobias to leave the room. At least for now. He glanced back at his sleeping wife, and his heart fluttered.

How did he get to this point so quickly? Tobias was not the marrying type, and yet, here he was – married to a wonderful woman he barely knew.

His heart bled for Emily. If she hadn't been kidnapped, she would have had nothing to do with the Jacobson gang, he was certain. The little he knew about them confirmed they kept to themselves when they were not stealing or killing victims. They were ghosts in the eyes of the law. They would disappear for weeks sometimes, then make their presence known by attacking yet another stagecoach. Usually one that was rumored to be carrying a large amount of gold.

From her own account, Emily was taken during a robbery. She would never have gone willingly, but had no choice.

His heart thudded.

Chapter Seventeen

As she opened her eyes, Emily wasn't sure how she's ended up in the bed. The last thing she remembered was sitting in front of the fire. She'd drifted off to sleep a few times throughout the evening.

The only explanation she could come up with, was Tobias carried her to bed. She was exhausted from everything that had happened the past few days. It was not surprising. Now though, it was morning, and she needed to get out of bed and cook breakfast for Tobias and their guests.

Moving quietly into the kitchen, Emily stoked the cookstove, and got the fire burning well. She would need it to cook the food, so she'd give it time. She then headed into the sitting room, for the same purpose.

She wasn't sure why, but didn't expect to find anyone there. Two of the marshals were there, and the fire was roaring. It made the room warm and cozy.

"Good morning, Mrs. Harrison," one of the marshals said.

That prompted the other marshal, who said the same. Emily was still trying to work out which marshal was which. She knew Peter Dodson, since he was first to arrive. The others? She couldn't remember which name belonged to which marshal.

She shrugged her shoulders. Did it really matter?

Emily knew it did. Everyone deserved respect, and knowing a person's name was only one way to do that. "Good morning to you both," she said. "I'll get coffee the moment the water boils." She headed back to the kitchen and pulled down six mugs in preparation. Emily then collected a large piece of bacon, which she would slice, and all the eggs left in the pantry.

To her dismay, there weren't enough eggs. "I…I need to collect eggs for breakfast," she told the marshals.

"I'm afraid that's not possible," one of the marshals told her. "You would be a sitting duck out there. Dillion can get them for you." He indicated for the other marshal to go, but Emily stopped him momentarily as she retrieved a basket. The marshal in question stared at it in despair, but took the basket nonetheless.

The sun was peeking out over the top of the horizon, and the sky was colorful. Emily loved this time of day, especially sitting out on the porch and watching as she sipped a mug of tea. It saddened her that she was no longer able to do this, but knew it was only temporary.

Lonnie Jacobson had a lot to answer for.

The thought angered her, but only momentarily. As much as Lonnie's actions had her locked down for as long as it took, this was not only for her, but for the safety of other potential victims as well. Not to mention past victims who no longer had a voice. Lonnie had to be stopped, and if that meant Emily had to stay inside until he was behind bars, so be it.

The moment the front door opened, Emily was filled with guilt. What if Lonnie was out there, and shot at the marshal? What if he killed the man? She would never forgive herself. Instead of wallowing in her guilt, she continued to slice the bacon. She had five hungry men to feed, and she couldn't keep them waiting.

The sizzle of the frying pan alerted her to the pan being hot enough to cook the bacon. She piled the bacon in there, then used the poker to move the logs around in the cookstove. She needed to refuel it, yet she didn't want to leave the bacon. It was a quandary, and Emily wasn't sure what to do.

She stood at the stove, ensuring the bacon didn't burn. Moments later Marshal Huggins returned with the basket half full of eggs. "I didn't break any," he said, his voice full of mirth.

Emily flashed him a brief smile, but said nothing.

Tobias entered the kitchen and gazed at her. "What's wrong?" he asked firmly. He always seemed to know when she was worried or unhappy.

"Nothing," she said, but he persisted. "The cookstove needs more fuel," she finally said. "I can't leave the food unattended."

He leaned in and kissed her cheek. "Consider it done," Tobias said. He fetched wood and kindling from the wood box in the sitting room. He then refilled the cookstove.

It seemed like such a small gesture, but Emily appreciated it more than anyone knew. "Thank you," she said when the fire was burning the way she needed it.

Once cooked, she moved the bacon to the oven, and began to crack the eggs. For all these men, she needed a lot, but using the eggs from yesterday and today, she still had enough left over to do some baking.

It seemed trivial to be thinking about baking, Emily knew, but it took her mind off her troubles. Especially worrying about the men who put their lives on the line for her. "Everyone sit," she demanded, and that included the marshals who had slept last night. Everyone crowded around the kitchen table, and Emily handed out their meals.

She watched their faces, and knew they appreciated the food she'd made. It was nice to see. Warmth flooded her as she sat down at the table with her own meal.

"This is good, Mrs. Harrison," Ethan Mercer said. "You're an excellent cook." He smiled at her then, and Emily felt as though she was contributing in some small way.

"Emily, please," she said firmly. "What you are doing is far more important," she told them. Her contribution was nothing compared to what these marshals were doing to keep her safe. "Anyone can cook."

"Without your good food, we couldn't do our jobs properly," Peter Dodson told her. He seemed to be the one in charge.

The others agreed, and Emily was filled with joy. According to Peter, she was making an important contribution. This morning she would make muffins, and perhaps another pound cake. They were sure to disappear quickly with all these hungry men around.

Chapter Eighteen

Tobias watched Emily as he ate. She put on a brave face, but it was clear she was worried. Not that he could blame her. She wouldn't be safe until Jacobson was either behind bars or no longer of this world.

What the outlaw had done was a hanging offense, and he deserved nothing less.

They might not have been married for long, or even known each other long, but Tobias had a soft spot for Emily. She'd been dealt a difficult hand and he wanted to fix it for her.

The stupidity of it was, Tobias wasn't sure he could. At least with four marshals here, they had a chance of catching the outlaw gang. Except that relied on the entire gang turning up together.

Tobias had a suspicion Lonnie was the only one involved in Emily's abduction and attempted murder. Even so, the others were complicit. They would likely receive the same treatment when caught. It sounded harsh, but Tobias knew they deserved nothing less.

Anger worked its way through his entire being. Tobias was not a man who angered easily. Working as a bodyguard all those years taught him to control his temper, and his emotions. This one hit close to home, and he couldn't help himself.

A warm hand slipped over his, and Tobias glanced up to find Emily studying him. Her eyes sad, she squeezed his hand. It was strangely comforting. A shiver went through him, but he managed to smile nonetheless.

They sat staring at each other like lovesick teenagers.

Tobias's heart thudded. He could not fall in love with Emily. They were strangers – he didn't know her, and she didn't know him. If it wasn't for tragedy, they would be unaware of each other's existence. Tobias drank down the last of his coffee, then stood. Emily glanced at him, a sad look on her face.

The current scenario was far from what he should be doing right now. Tobias didn't care. He was here for a reason. Now he knew what it was.

It wasn't to undertake his job as a lumberjack – any able-bodied man could do it. Fate brought him here. Fate had also put him in the right place at the right time. He was glad it had, otherwise Emily would be laying on the undertaker's slab at this very moment.

The thought had his heart shattering. How did he become so endeared to this woman so quickly?

Chapter Nineteen

Emily followed Tobias's lead and stood. She collected the soiled dishes and began to restore order to the kitchen. Stacking the plates in the sink, something, she wasn't sure what, had her gazing out across the paddock. Her eyes trained on the slight movement. It was difficult to decipher at this time of day. Everywhere she looked, Emily saw shadows.

"Tobias," she whispered. "I think…" She took a deep breath and let it out slowly. "I think Lonnie's out there. In the shadows." Emily pointed in the direction she believed Lonnie to be located.

Silence filled the room.

Without warning, the four marshals were on their feet. Peter Dodson was barking out orders. Soon three men were running out the door, guns in hand.

Peter stayed behind, to add another layer of protection, he said. Despite Tobias's objections, Peter still stayed. This was a fight for the marshals, and nothing Tobias said could change his mind.

Emily appreciated him staying, but it didn't sit well with Tobias. She watched as he stared out the window. "I don't see anyone except the marshals," he said, then put an arm around her. As much as Emily appreciated him comforting her, she knew what she'd seen.

"Oh, he's there," she said, her voice low. "Perhaps…what if he's been there all along, waiting for his chance to try to kill me again." Emily knew she sounded somewhat hysterical, but wouldn't anyone under the circumstances?

Peter Dodson joined them at the window. He studied the area, then turned to Emily. "If you believe you saw Jacobson, I trust you did. He is as slippery as a snake, and we've been trying to catch Jacobson and his gang for years." Peter took a breath, and let it out slowly. "We *will* get him this time. The outlaw has become dangerous and unpredictable. How long were you with him?" he asked Emily.

She closed her eyes momentarily. "With him?" Emily shook her head. "I was never *with* him. The man abused me every chance he got."

The marshal studied her. He nodded briefly but said not a word. He glanced at Tobias, and the two men seemed to have an understanding of her situation.

"Emily," Tobias said quietly. "Why didn't you tell me?"

Tears came to her eyes but Emily refused to let them fall. She wiped at her eyes, but it didn't help. She relived the terror, even if it was only in her mind. She could never utter them out loud. Humiliated and abused – that's what she endured with Lonnie Jacobson.

On her way to visit an elderly aunt, Lonnie and the Jacobson gang intercepted the stagecoach. They stole gold and anything else of value. Before they left, Lonnie turned to her and licked his lips. Then he snatched Emily right out of her seat.

As he rode away, holding her far closer than was respectable, he told Emily, she was to be his slave. She cringed at the laughter in his voice.

And that's exactly what happened – she was his slave in every way. Whatever Lonnie wanted, Lonnie got. At the very moment he wanted it. To disobey Lonnie, was to be punished in ways Emily never dreamed possible.

Without warning, gunfire rang out. Emily glanced about, looking for Lonnie. Was he shot, or was he the one doing the shooting? She knew Lonnie would not shoot unless he was confident he could hit his target.

Suddenly the room seemed chaotic. She was being lifted and carried into another room. "Get under the bed and stay there," Tobias demanded.

Emily was fuming. "You could have just said so," she said, her voice full of bitterness. Over the past days, she was treated as though she didn't exist. Too many people telling her what to do, and Emily didn't like it one bit. "If you give me a gun, I can help," she said, her voice demanding now.

How dare they tell her what to do and where to go. She didn't want to hide under the bed. Instead she wanted to help.

"No way," Tobias said firmly. "You're more likely to be killed than to help."

Typical. She shouldn't have expected anything less. As the gunfire rang out, Tobias shoved her underneath the bed. "Stay there," he demanded, this time his voice full of anger. "It's for your own good." He turned and left the room.

Still fuming, Emily slid out from under the bed. She quickly fashioned her hair into a tight bun at the back of her head, then sat on the edge of the bed. Why was it men automatically assumed women were useless when it came to their own safety? Especially when it came to using firearms.

She stormed out of the room, and went straight to the kitchen where Tobias and Peter were the last time she saw them. It was then she discovered Tobias was using a handgun, not the rifle he'd held earlier.

Good. That meant it was likely hanging on the rack over the fire in the sitting room.

~*~

Still fuming, but trying to calm herself, Emily sat on the sofa in the sitting room. That positioned her opposite the front door. Should anyone, Lonnie or one of his brothers, breach the door, she wouldn't hesitate to shoot. Despite the men surrounding her, it didn't feel right to let them fight alone.

Her mind was full of bravado, but Emily wasn't sure she could shoot another person. Except when that person was trying to kill her. Should Lonnie throw open the door, she would shoot first and ask questions later.

She pulled up her sleeves, heart pounding, and waited for the inevitable. She had eight rounds in the chamber, and a full box sitting beside her. She hadn't taken long to find the bullets for the rifle. Tobias was predictable in that respect.

It had been a while since she'd handled a rifle, but it was something you never forgot.

Chapter Twenty

Tobias stood next to Peter Dodson at the kitchen window. Something didn't feel right, and he couldn't shake the feeling. At least he knew Emily was safe underneath the bed.

A shiver went down his spine. Why was he feeling this way? Surely his wife would stay hidden as he'd demanded.

Except Emily didn't like being told what to do. He raced into the bedroom. Emily was nowhere to be seen. His heart pounded as panic overcame him. How could Lonnie Jacobson have gotten into the cottage and taken Emily without anyone knowing?

He felt lightheaded at the thought. Tobias sat on the edge of the bed while he cleared his head. What would Emily do in this situation? Would she stay put, like he told her? Tobias dropped to the floor and checked the place he'd left her.

He was ashamed to admit he hadn't swept underneath the bed for some time, which worked in his favor. Staring at the markings, he could see Emily had slipped out from under the bed after he'd left the room. He followed the dusty footprints. His heart was still pounding, but he no longer believed she'd been taken.

Why she would leave the safe haven he'd given her, Tobias didn't know, but he was pretty sure he knew where she would be.

Stepping quietly, he headed for the sitting room. Glancing up, he could see his rifle was gone. It was then he spotted Emily sitting opposite the door, waiting for Lonnie to enter. What if one of the marshals came in and she shot them? It would be a tragedy.

"Emily," he said quietly, trying not to startle her. "What are you doing?"

She turned her head to face him. But only for mere moments. "What does it look like?" The determination on her face worried him. Had she even held a rifle before? "Go back to the kitchen. I'm fine here," she told him firmly.

Instead, Tobias sat down beside her on the sofa. "Jacobson wouldn't be so stupid as to try and get in through the front door." He put an arm around Emily, but she shook it away.

Instead of complying as he'd hoped, she huffed at him. "I know Lonnie better than anyone. Except maybe his brothers," she said as she tightened her grip on the rifle butt.

"Do you even know how to shoot?" he asked gently, already knowing the answer would be no.

Emily stared at him. "Of course I have. I was brought up on a ranch. With no sons to take over, it was all up to me."

Her words shocked him. "So what? You're a cowboy?" He chuckled then, finding it funny all of a sudden. "If that's the case, how did Jacobson get his hands on you?"

"My mother wanted me to visit with my aunt, and *learn to be a lady*." She rolled her eyes then, and Tobias found it amusing, but held back his laughter. She was, after all, holding a fully loaded rifle. "My parents wanted me to marry, but Mother said I wasn't *polished* enough." Emily rolled her eyes again.

She obviously did not agree with her parents. Especially since she was a grown woman. Emily had to be in her early thirties, he was certain – why were her parents pressuring her? He was confused at first, but realized they wanted an heir for the ranch.

Emily didn't seem like the sort to argue, at least with her parents. He knew though, if they hadn't forced her to travel, then she wouldn't be in this predicament. Still, they weren't to know.

The door handle rattled, then the door flew open. Emily lifted the rifle, and Tobias pointed his gun at the men entering the cottage.

"Don't shoot!" The words sounded urgent, and so they should be. The three marshals stood in the doorway. "He's out there alright," Ben Delaney said. "But we couldn't entice them into the open. Not that I blame them."

Dillion Huggins spoke. "I believe I hit one of them, but he's still alive."

Peter Dodson entered the sitting room and demanded a report. "How many are out there?" he wanted to know.

"I believe the entire gang are here," Ethan Mercer said. "I'm pretty sure they've realized Emily is here, alive and well. Otherwise, why would they converge on Tobias's cottage?"

It was a fair question, and Tobias had no choice but to agree. Emily studied him. No longer determined, she now appeared worried.

Suddenly she smirked. "Ha! They think I am helpless. I've got news for them." She lifted the rifle once more, and pointed it toward the door.

Tobias stared at Peter Dobson, who shook his head ever so slightly. Tobias almost missed it, the movement was so slight. The marshal silently indicated for Tobias to follow him, and they ended up in the kitchen.

His heart pounding, Tobias stared out the window. Were the Jacobson gang out there, waiting to pounce?

"Did you know your wife could shoot? Or that she was so determined?" Peter asked, doubt written all over his face.

Tobias was shell-shocked. "None of that. Until a few minutes ago, she was placid and compliant. You saw it for yourself." He wiped a hand across his unshaven chin, fear abruptly hitting him. Not for himself, but for Emily. Anyone who walked through that door were targets for her rage.

She had a rifle, his rifle, and she knew how to use it. Tobias would rather see the Jacobson gang arrested and tried for their actions. Killing them was too quick, and meant they avoided the punishment they deserved. It was clear Emily wanted to dish out her own form of punishment, but it would forever play on her mind.

"What are you two whispering about back here?" Emily's voice rang throughout the kitchen. The two men suddenly turned to see Emily behind them, the rifle still in her hands, but at a safe angle.

Tobias glanced at Peter then back at his wife. "I need coffee. I was about to fill the kettle." He reached across as though he was about to do exactly that, but she scowled.

"That's a lie," she snapped, then moved closer to the stove. "Hold this," she demanded, and handed Tobias the rifle.

He glanced at Peter who raised his eyebrows. Tobias had seen this before, it was a reaction to the stress of the situation. Except it was worse given Emily knew how to handle a firearm. The hardest part now, was knowing what to do. Should he confiscate the rifle, and force her to act more ladylike, or hand the rifle back to her once she finished making coffee?

Tobias knew it was a dilemma, and no matter which way he went, he knew the consequences could be dire.

Chapter Twenty-One

Emily fumed. She *knew* those two were not making coffee. Instead, they were scheming. She was certain they were making decisions about her life. About how to handle her in regards to the rifle.

Men were not used to women being self sufficient, or to them being confident and competent with firearms.

She grew up with men like that.

Instead of arguing, she just went about her business making coffee. If that appeased them, so be it.

It was her fault, Emily knew it was. After what Lonnie did to her she was completely drained and helpless. Except now she wasn't. She would do her utmost to defend herself, even if Tobias and the marshals didn't think she should. Or could.

She saw the looks on their faces when they saw what she held in her hands. She also knew what they would be thinking – that she couldn't handle it, or wouldn't use it. Emily believed she was probably far more competent with a firearm than any of them.

A hand landed on her shoulder, and Emily spun around, ready to attack. Except it was Tobias, not Lonnie. The shocked look on his face made her cringe. She was still living with the after effects of her abduction. It was not surprising.

She had no intention of becoming a wallflower, simply because it's what these men, especially her husband, believed that's what she should be.

She was a strong and confident woman. Raised by a strong and confident woman. Her father wasn't completely on board with her being taught to live like a man, but he never had the courage to say no to her mother. Emily was pleased about that.

"Emily," Tobias said quietly, then pulled her close to his chest. Did he think she couldn't cope? Did he see her as incompetent when it came to defending herself? His arm around her soothed Emily's frayed edges. Not completely, but it did help. She glanced up into his face, and he smiled. Except the smile didn't reach his eyes, telling her he was covering up his own emotions for her.

Instead of telling him so, she snuggled into him. Tobias tightened his grip on her, and caressed her cheek. It felt good, but Emily didn't want him to believe she was weak. She was far from it. He leaned in and kissed her forehead. "I need to finish making coffee," she whispered, and he loosened his grip enough for her to slide out.

His warmth disappeared, and it made her sad. Tobias said nothing, but his face said it all – he didn't want her to leave his arms. For someone who didn't want her, he seemed disappointed she'd left his side.

"There's still some pound cake," she announced, and added it to a large plate. "I need to do some cooking," she said to no one in particular. For the men, they needed their bellies full, but for Emily she needed to keep busy. She hated to stand around doing nothing when her cooking was just as important as those men yielding guns.

She shook her head briefly. If only she'd realized what Lonnie was up to when the stagecoach was robbed. Emily was certain she could have overwhelmed him, but his attack on her came out of the blue. None of his brothers participated in her abduction, and moved back from the coach as though declaring they had no part in it. They had stopped Lonnie choking her, too.

As she poured the boiling water into the cups, something outside caught Emily's eye. She momentarily stared out the kitchen window, trying to process exactly what it was she saw. The movement stopped – as though whoever, or whatever it was saw her watching. "Pssst, Tobias," she said quietly, as though whoever was out there could hear here. "You too, Peter. What is that outside?" Emily didn't point. She also gave no indication she'd seen the movement.

It was stupid, Emily knew it was. Except if it was Lonnie, he now knew for certain she was inside the cottage. She was watching him watching her. It wasn't a good feeling, not even a little bit. Emily's heart thudded. "Where is that rifle?" she demanded, feeling suddenly flustered. She moved away from the window, and suggested the others do the same.

Without warning, Peter hurried into the sitting room. Emily heard him muttering, but didn't know what he was saying. He was probably barking out orders, as he often did. No matter what he was saying, it wasn't relevant to her. Emily knew what she was going to do, and no one was going to stop her.

Lonnie Jacobson had to be stopped, and it looked like she was the one to do it.

"Coffee and cake is on the table," Emily said when she entered the sitting room, rifle by her side.

Tobias was still in the kitchen, and Peter had rejoined him. All three marshals hesitated, then two left the room. Dillion Huggins hung back. "What are you up to?" he demanded of the new bride. He studied her but Emily stood her ground, saying nothing. "Whatever it is, Peter didn't approve it, I'm certain."

Emily's sense of independence kicked in. "No, he didn't, but it's not his choice. Tobias tells me there's a loft in the barn. I am going to visit the barn cat and her kittens. Most of all, it should be a decent place to see if Lonnie tries to get into the cottage. One shot and he is taken care of." By *taken care of,* she really meant he would be dead, except she was too much of a lady to say it out loud.

"I…I don't know," Dillion said. "Peter would have my hide if I let you do that alone. We're supposed to be protecting you, not the other way around."

"As a matter of fact," Emily said firmly, "I understood you were here to arrest the Jacobson gang. Protecting me, as I understand it, is secondary." Emily hurried to the front door and unlocked it. Moments later she was outside and headed to the loft of Tobias's barn, rifle in hand, and a pocket full of ammunition.

~*~

As she climbed the ladder to the loft, Emily knew her actions were bordering on stupidity. But she also knew she couldn't continue to live in fear. Except it wasn't all about her, it was also about five men, who she barely knew but were putting their lives on the line for her.

"Emily," Dillion said firmly, "you need to go back inside. Goodness knows who is up there."

She glanced back at him, as he stood at the bottom of the stairs. Dillion was beyond worried, he was distressed. Whether he was worried for her, for himself, or the repercussions of letting her get out of the cottage, she didn't know. What she did know was it had to be done.

Sitting around waiting for something to happen was not her style. She'd been brought up to do whatever was needed, and nothing less. She hurried up the last couple of rungs, and glanced about. It was all clear except for mama cat and her babies. The scene before her melted Emily's heart. They were so sweet.

She was about to put down the rifle when she heard movement, and it wasn't the marshal coming up behind her. It was up here in the loft. Dillion must have heard it too because he was beside her in a flash.

"Emily, sweet Emily," Lonnie said as he revealed himself. "You are supposed to be dead."

"And you are about to be," Emily said firmly, gripping the rifle and pointing it in his direction. Her heart thudded and her head was spinning from the stress of the situation. She had never been in such a position before, but she was not about to let Lonnie get away with what he'd done to her.

Her finger on the trigger, Emily was ready. Standing next to her, Dillion whispered for her to drop to the floor. She pretended not to hear.

Lonnie lifted his gun and aimed it at Emily. He was going to finish her off this time, she was certain. Gunshots rang out in the large barn. Her ears rang, and she dropped to the hay covered floor. Dillion fell down too.

Emily was confused – she'd only heard the one gunshot. She gingerly lifted her head, and saw Lonnie laying on the hay, his chest covered in blood.

Chapter Twenty-Two

Tobias saw Emily drop to the floor moments after he took the kill shot. His heart shattered. Did Jacobson shoot her before Tobias could stop him?

He was furious with her. What sort of fool move was that, coming out here without telling anyone? Except they couldn't find Huggins, so Tobias assumed he'd tried to stop her and had ended up accompanying her for Emily's own protection.

He hurried up the ladder and was on the loft far quicker than he ever had before. His eyes scanned the area. Jacobson was down, but so was Huggins and Emily. His heart thudded. Did that mean Jacobson killed them before he'd shot the outlaw?

Running across to the pair who lay flat on the hay, he breathed a sigh of relief to see Emily's head bob up. Huggins had an arm across her back, holding her down. The marshal was suddenly on his feet, gun still in his hand, and hurried across to where the outlaw lay. He removed Jacobson's gun, then checked his pulse. "He's gone," Huggins said, with no sign of emotion on his face.

It was then he noticed Tobias. "Any sign of the brothers?" he asked Tobias.

Tobias shook his head, more to clear his thoughts than to answer the question. "They are out there somewhere," he said, then hurried over to his wife. Helping Emily to her feet, his anger began to melt. "I thought you were dead," he whispered, then pulled her close, fighting back tears of relief.

Wrapping her in his arms, Tobias felt his heartbeat begin to slow. He lifted her chin with his fingers and gazed into her eyes. "Don't you ever do something like that again," he said firmly, then kissed her on the lips for the very first time.

In that moment, he knew he couldn't live without her, and the bride that was forced on him only days ago, was his soulmate. Tobias only hoped he was hers.

~*~

Three of the four marshals were outside, tying Jacobson's dead body to their buckboard. They moved it forward to ensure the rest of the gang saw that Lonnie was dead. It was to be a warning to them all.

Sitting on the sofa next to his wife, Tobias tried to dispel all his anger at her. He swore he would stay until the four brothers were in custody.

Emily stood, and turned to Tobias. "I'll make coffee," she said quietly. "I think we all deserve it." Grabbing her hand as she tried to leave, Tobias wasn't certain he wanted her to leave his side. Not after the events of not long ago. His heartbeat had slowed, but was still quicker than normal. He'd experienced this before. Back when he worked as a bodyguard.

The truth of the matter was, he was working as a bodyguard, this time for his wife. All the details were the same, except for being paid for doing the job. His payment this time was love. At least he hoped it was.

He heard Emily rattling around in the kitchen. It sounded like she was doing more than making coffee. He needed to investigate.

The aroma of muffins or cake, or something delicious, hit him the closer he got. Emily was right when she said baking took her mind off her situation. She appeared so much calmer now than she had a short time ago.

He moved closer to her, and wrapped Emily in his arms. She didn't resist, and he reveled in her nearness. What he wouldn't do to make theirs a real marriage. The thought had him reeling. What if she wanted to annul their marriage now that Jacobson was out of the picture? From what she'd said, the brothers were not her concern. They'd even tried to save her from their older brother.

Still, Tobias needed to know they were locked up, and no longer a threat.

"Smells good," he said, still holding her close. At that moment, something overcame him. At first he didn't recognize it, then it hit him, and Tobias almost reeled backwards from the revelation. "I think l Iove you, Emily. I never want to lose you."

She pulled away from him, and glazed up into Tobias's face. "We…we haven't known each other very long," she whispered. "And yet, I feel the same way. At least I have feelings for you, Tobias," she said, then leaned into him again.

This was the happiest Tobias had felt in a very long time.

The pair stood in each other's arms for what seemed an eternity. They only broke apart when Emily had to check the muffins she had cooking. She turned to reach for a kitchen towel. "Well, I'll be…" she began.

Tobias followed her line of sight. Was he seeing things? The four remaining members of the Jacobson gang were striding toward the cottage, trampling through the thick snow, their hands in the air, and guns holstered. "I didn't think they would give up this easily," Tobias said, still not truly believing what he saw.

He dashed out of the kitchen and ran into the sitting room. "Peter," he said still not believing it. "You have to see this." All four marshals followed him.

"Could be a trap," Peter said as he stared at the brothers who appeared to be surrendering.

Tobias had seen a lot of things in his life, but nothing like this. "Could be, but I don't think so," he said, hoping and praying he wasn't wrong.

The four marshals were gone before Tobias could say another word. He watched out the window, Emily by his side, as the four men were handcuffed and taken into custody.

Chapter Twenty-Three

The relief Emily felt was palpable. Never in her life did she believe such a thing was possible. In the short time she'd been held hostage by the gang, it was clear Lonnie was in charge. The only time he'd listened to any of his brothers was when he'd tried to strangle her. And that was only because it was making them uncomfortable, she was certain.

With all four Jacobson gang members secured on the back of the buckboard along with their dead brother, the marshals packed up the little they'd brought with them and drove away. But not until Emily had packed up enough muffins for them all, including the Jacobson gang.

She honestly didn't know why she'd done that. Except Emily did. They had saved her life. If not for them, Lonnie would have strangled her in front of them all. Her hands went to her throat. The bruising was almost gone, and barely visible. No one had mentioned it, so she didn't either.

As the buckboard drove away, Emily sank against her husband. The man she'd fallen in love with over these past days. Never did she believe it was possible for her to feel this way about someone she'd only recently met.

She gazed up at him. Her lumberjack husband. The man who didn't want to marry. Or should she say, didn't want to marry her.

For all she knew, Tobias could have a girlfriend. Someone he truly loved. Was she keeping him from the love of his life? His true soulmate? The thought made her heart hurt.

"We don't have to stay married, if that's what you want," Emily whispered.

Tobias stared at her. "You want an annulment?" His voice was barely audible and he appeared distressed. She might as well have slapped him for the pain he seemed to be feeling.

Her heart twisted and her chest hurt. She'd become used to having Tobias by her side – could she live without him? That really was the only thing that mattered. Tobias said he thought he loved her, not that he actually did love her. Emily knew she had feelings for him, but was it love? Were they actually in love, or was it the stress of the situation? There was only one way to find out.

And that was to leave him.

~*~

Emily sat at the window of her hotel watching the world go by. She loved this little town. Mountain Pass had saved her from certain death. Except that was untrue. Tobias, her sweet husband, had saved her. If not for him, she would not be here now.

How he'd managed to kill Lonnie from where he stood down in the barn, she would never know. He was an experienced marksman, she'd learned that much.

If not for her, danger would not have been brought to the area, and Tobias would not have been forced to marry her. Everything that was wrong with this scenario centered around Emily and her attempted murder.

Her eyes filled with tears. Everything that happened was her fault. She knew it, but Tobias refused to admit it. He said it was all on Lonnie. He was right of course, but without her in the mix, it wouldn't have come to this.

Emily swiped at her eyes. She was finally able to access her bank account without worrying about Lonnie finding her.

Checking the clock on the wall, Emily knew it was time to leave. Today was the trial of the remaining four Jacobson gang members. She was expected to give evidence, and as much as Emily knew she was the only living witness, she didn't want to tell her story for all to hear.

She wondered if Tobias would be there. Emily hoped he wasn't, otherwise, she might change her mind and go back to him. Except they planned to arrange an annulment after the trial. Everything had been chaotic after the arrests, and they decided to wait. Hence the reason she was living out of a boarding house.

It wasn't like being home. Tobias's cottage had become home to her, but that all changed when Emily moved to town. He had tried to convince her to stay, but she was certain he was only saying it to make her feel better.

Except she felt worse. There was nothing here that made her feel like she belonged. The bed had been slept on by dozens of women. The chair sat in by many, and she was convinced they'd all sat at the window and watched people go by, just as she was doing now.

A knock at the door startled her. "Mrs. Harrison!" the voice said abruptly.

Emily hurried to the door, and opened it. "Mrs. Granger, is something wrong?" The boarding house owner studied her. "Your *husband* is downstairs. You know how I feel about men frequenting these rooms."

Fighting the urge to roll her eyes, Emily straightened her shoulders, and followed the older woman down the stairs.

Tobias stood staring out onto the street. Emily's heart fluttered. It had only been a matter of days since she moved to town, but Emily missed him more than she could say. "Tobias." As she spoke his name, something inside of her shifted. He turned to face her, his features strained, but forced a smile to his face.

"I came to accompany you to the trial," Tobias said, his voice full of emotion. As she almost reached the bottom of the stairs, he reached out and took her hand. A shiver went down her spine at his gentle touch.

Emily stared up into his honey colored eyes. If they had children, their eyes might be that same beautiful color.

Emily shook the thought away. She was trying to distance herself from her husband, not endear herself to him. Once the trial was over, they would apply for an annulment, and she would be free to go wherever she wanted.

Only she didn't want to leave Mountain Pass. Doing so meant she would never see Tobias again.

"Emily?" His voice seemed miles away, but his touch was oh so gentle. Her head was spinning and her heart racing. The next thing she knew, Emily was cradled in her husband's arms.

Just the way she liked it.

~*~

The doc checked her over and declared Emily was overwhelmed by the stress of the trial. Tobias accompanied her there, and held her hand as she gave her version of events. She spoke about how the Jacobson men stopped Lonnie from strangling her. That they were unable to stop him dumping her in the cold and snow, was not their fault. Tobias was called to the stand for a statement about his part in Emily's rescue.

Having to relive that day, and listening to Tobias explain how he'd found her, and what condition she was in was heartbreaking. Her eyes filled with tears, and once Tobias finished, he took her outside, away from the sadness.

Tobias held her in his arms and comforted her, and Emily knew that was exactly where she needed to be. Where she wanted to be. She loved him too much to let him go. Except it was dependent on Tobias. He might not want her back.

She glanced up at him, then caressed his cheek. Tobias leaned down and stared into her face. "I've missed you," he whispered, then leaned closer, as if ready to kiss her. He hesitated, waiting for her permission.

"Hurry up and kiss me," Emily said, and that's exactly what Tobias did.

Chapter Twenty-Four

The trial was over in less than a day. The Jacobson gang admitted their crimes. They asked Emily to forgive them for not stopping Lonnie. She complied, much to Tobias disgust. Still, it was her choice, and he didn't try to dissuade her. It was nearly Christmas after all; a time of generosity and giving.

Instead he took her to the diner for a meal, where they talked about an annulment. The moment the words were out, Emily's eyes filled with tears. "Is that what *you* want?" she asked quietly as she pushed food around her plate.

It was far from what he wanted, but the subject had to be breached. She had let him kiss her, but that meant nothing. Emily was anxious after what she'd endured. Not only the trial, but making her statement, and having to face the four Jacobson gang members.

She was a strong woman, there was no doubt about it. It was the reason Tobias was certain she would want her independence. It broke his heart to even think about the possibility. He shook his head. "It's not, and I think you know it." He ran a hand through his hair, his irritation growing by the minute.

Emily studied him. Her blue eyes penetrated his, and it was as though she could see all the way to his soul.

She slid her hand across the table to cover his. "We were forced into this marriage. I knew from the start it wasn't what you wanted. I didn't want it either."

He had to acknowledge she was right. "That's true," he said quietly, "But things are different now."

"In what way?" Emily continued to study him, and Tobias felt uncomfortable as a result. She squeezed his hand and a shiver went down his spine. He had never felt this way about any woman, but his wife did strange things to him. Tobias licked his lips and opened his mouth, but didn't know what to say. This was a whole new scenario for him. "You said you had feelings for me. Or have you forgotten?"

Warmth filled him at the memory. He'd let his guard down, but knew his words were genuine. It wasn't the heat of the moment, and it wasn't the stress he was under. It was an unadulterated fact. "I haven't forgotten. I love you," he whispered. "I live a primitive life. Nothing fancy." He turned his face away, not wanting to see her reaction.

He heard Emily's intake of breath. "I want to live that simple life with you," she said. "Lonnie is dead, and the remaining members of the Jacobson gang will be old men when they are released from jail. If they last that long. They are no longer a threat." She stood and went around to the other side of the table where Tobias sat. Emily stared into his eyes. "I love you more than life itself, Tobias Harrison. If we weren't already married, I would march you into the church right now, and demand Preacher Chalmers marry us."

"This close to Christmas?" Tobias asked, then chuckled. His wife meant the world to him, and he would marry her all over again if that was what made her happy.

 Epilogue

Three years later…

Emily stood at the window, staring out across the paddock. Tobias knew what she was thinking – her memory of that day Lonnie Jacobson tried to kill her in the loft, was still vivid. The snow covered trees and grass mimicked the way it was that day as well. It was only days until Christmas, just as it was now.

Tobias stepped toward her, and wrapped his wife in his arms. There was little more he could do for her except love her and assure her she was safe.

"Papa, me too."

Tobias leaned down and picked up two year old Dillion – named after the marshal who protected his wife when she foolishly made herself a target.

Snow covered much of the empty paddock, telling Tobias Christmas was nearly here. This year, Christmas would be extra special. At one-year-old, Dillion didn't understand Christmas, or his presents. This Christmas would be far different.

"I need to finish this," Emily whispered, indicating the cookies she was making especially for the day of celebration.

"You need to rest," Tobias told her sternly. His hand slipped to her swollen belly, and Dillion followed suit.

"Baby," Dillion said, then smiled at his parents. "Down, Papa," he added, then ran over to the Christmas tree the moment his feet hit the floor. The two-year-old had helped decorate the small tree – one they had found together as a family. It was small, compact, chosen to fit the sitting room without overtaking the entire space.

The fire roared. The crackles of the logs was always a comfort to Tobias. His wife said she loved it too. It made him wonder if that was because her life had been saved by the heat of the fire.

Dillion stared out the window, seemingly mesmerized. His father joined the young boy. "Look Papa, deer," he said. Tobias joined the boy at the window and lifted him to ensure Dillion had a better view.

Tobias put his fingers to his lips. "Don't scare the deer," he whispered, and his son nodded his compliance.

A few things had changed since the day the Jacobson gang were caught. The biggest change was expanding the cottage to accommodate their growing family. Never in his wildest dreams did Tobias believe he would one day have a wife, let alone a family.

"Baby's kicking," Emily said, entering the sitting room. "Oh. What are you looking at?" she asked.

"It's a deer, Mama," Dillion said, turning to face her, a huge smile on his face.

Tobias glanced at the snow through the window. "Who would like to build a snowman?" he asked, only to be met by squeals from his son. It would be freezing out there, but they would rug up to keep warm.

He turned to Emily, but felt certain she wouldn't want to go out in her condition. "I'm not coming," she told them. "But I will have warm cocoa and cookies waiting when you come back."

Dillion was so excited and did a little dance as he continued to watch the deer frolicking nearby.

Outside, the pair worked together to build their snowman. It might be a little small, but was just the right size for Dillion. They added a scarf around his neck, a carrot for his nose, and sticks for his arms. Emily had given them a handful of old buttons for the snowman's eyes and shirt.

Once finished, Tobias scooped up his son and stepped back to admire their handiwork. He silently admitted it might not be the best snowman he'd ever seen, but it was made with love.

Hurrying back inside, the pair went straight to the fire. Tobias held Dillion's tiny hands in wonderment. He glanced around the cottage. It was very different to the way it used to be – bland and unwelcoming.

With Emily's help, it had become a home, instead of place to simply eat and lay his head. Their home was filled with love. Tobias couldn't believe there was once a time he did not welcome Emily as his wife.

Now he didn't know what he would do without her.

From the Author

Thank you so much for reading my book – I hope you enjoyed it.

I would greatly appreciate you leaving a review where you purchased, even if it is only a one-liner. It helps to have my books more visible!

About the Author

Multi-published, award-winning and bestselling author Cheryl Wright, former secretary, debt collector, account manager, writing coach, and shopping tour hostess, loves reading.

She writes historical romantic suspense and historical western romance.

She lives in Melbourne, Australia, and is married with two adult children and has six grandchildren, and twin great-grandchildren.

When she's not writing, she can be found in her craft room making greeting cards.

Links

Website: *http://www.cheryl-wright.com/*

Facebook Reader Group:
*https://www.facebook.com/groups/cherylwrightaut
hor/*

Join My Newsletter:

https://cheryl-wright.com/newsletter/
(and receive a free book)